The Last Water-hole

When ex-outlaw Bobbie Lee sees a rider approaching Beattie's Halt he know it means trouble. Hours later his innocent son is gunned down in the saloon and three more hard-bitten strangers have joined the gunman called Van Gelderen. But who are they?

Two days later a second young man dies and the strangers leave town. But murder cannot go unpunished. Bobbie Lee, Will Blunt and his daughter, Cassie, pick up the trail outside Beattie's Halt. In the scorching heat of the desert old feuds are settled in a six-gun blaze.

The Last Water-hole

JACK SHERIFF

A Black Horse Western

ROBERT HALE · LONDON

ISBN-10: 0-7090-8152-9
ISBN-13: 978-0-7090-8152-4

Robert Hale Limited
Clerkenwell House
Clerkenwell Green
London EC1R 0HT

Typeset by
Derek Doyle & Associates, Shaw Heath
Printed and bound in Great Britain by
Antony Rowe Limited, Wiltshire

PART ONE

THE RIDER

ONE

Bobbie Lee saw the distant rider when he was out watching his son, Jason, swilling the wide gallery that fronted The Last Water-hole saloon. Sweat was dripping from the 16-year old's smooth chin as he threw the last bucket of soapy water over warped boards already steaming in the blistering sun. But he was grinning, his vacant blue eyes alight, his pleasure clear as he performed just about the one task that didn't tax his simple mind.

Only maybe seeing the distant rider is the wrong way to put it, Bobbie Lee thought, as the black dot darted about like an annoying speck in the eye and the heat-haze shimmered against the dazzling white of the landscape transforming everything a man saw into a quivering, dancing mirage.

But he was there, no doubt about it. And alone.

Bobbie Lee stepped out of the way with a grin as Jason charged past with the empty bucket and thumped into the saloon. He watched the lad disappear into the shadows, then went to the rail and fired up a smoke. The drying boards creaked

7

underfoot. The wooden rail that looked like it might have been painted, oh, maybe five years ago by someone who was half asleep at the time, was hot under his hands. He stood there, smoking, gazing contemplatively at his surroundings.

Thirty yards away, across a rutted expanse of white dust that served as a square, the sprawling shack that was Chip Morgan's general store was like a derelict ship on a sea of sand. Morgan, in work pants and grey undershirt, was using hammer and six-inch nails on an outbuilding that over the summer had become detached from the main premises. As his wife, Alice, watched from the doorway with hands on hips, the store owner's curses – almost drowning the thud and ring of the hammer – were like the coughing of a sick coyote.

Some way off to the east, Will Blunt's farm was a cluster of four long, low-slung sheds and empty corrals that brought the sum total of the buildings in Beattie's Halt to six – though what the hell Will and his wife, Beth, managed to farm in that godforsaken spot Bobbie Lee never had figured out in the twelve months since he rode into the halt and took over the run-down saloon.

And just how long Blunt's daughter, Cassie, was going to put up with the old cowman's cantanker-ous ways before jumping on her paint pony and pointing it towards the nearest big town was anybody's guess.

There were certainly enough guesses being tossed around. Chip Morgan had two sons, Zeke and Ed. Both of those strapping fellers had courted Cassie Blunt, both had been sent packing to speculate on her future and how it meshed – or didn't mesh – with theirs. Because it didn't make sense for the one young – or medium young – woman in the Halt to stay around if she wasn't going to wed and settle down.

But she had stayed. And the boys? Well, they'd decided that, for them, the Halt held no future at all; he'd been told that both of them had ridden away a couple of years ago at the end of a long winter. As far as Bobbie Lee knew, Zeke had headed East to make his fortune and Ed was working as wrangler or cowpoke on a ranch in southern Texas. Maybe they'd return, maybe not. If they did, they'd need ambition laced with a healthy slug of resilience if they were to do anything with a decaying settlement that was little more than a dusty ghost town.

Bobbie Lee drew on the cigarette, blew out a stream of smoke. He gazed towards Blunt's farm, thought he saw the bright glint of Cassie's flaxen hair but decided with some disappointment that it was just another mirage.

Which thought swung Bobbie Lee's attention back to the distant rider. He squinted into the sun, looking beyond the tall, rickety windmill with its stationary vanes, across the water-tank that was two-thirds empty; across the peeled poles of the fence that Blunt had started one summer but never got around to finishing, and off into the near distance.

Yep. One rider. Comin' in nice and easy like he

was a feller considering the welfare of his horse. Not pushing. Looked like maybe he'd come across from San Angelo way, followed the Middle Concho and was now set back on his heels – in a manner of speaking – by the realization that what lay ahead of him were the daunting hundred-foot-high bluffs and buttresses that marked the edge of the vast, empty wilderness of the Llano Estacado: the Staked Plains.

Any man looking to cross that in midsummer, Bobbie Lee thought with amused cynicism, has got a posse hammering along his back trail or something mighty enticing up ahead, because in between where he is and where he's going there sure as hell is a whole lot of nothing.

And in that moment, out of nowhere, Bobbie Lee knew this man was trouble.

Distance being deceptive, it took the man a full half hour to reach Beattie's Halt. By then the gallery's board floor was bone-dry and bleached white, Chip Morgan had flung the shiny hammer in the direction of Blunt's empty corrals and come sweating and muttering across the expanse of dust, and he and Bobbie Lee were perched on stools on the customer's side of the rough timber bar with glasses of tepid beer clutched in their big fists.

In the restful shadows on the edge of the sunlight shafting through the windows, they stared at nothing as the stranger tied his horse at the rail and clomped up the steps; out of the corner of their eyes saw his shadow stretch long across the sawdust as the door swung open and he stood motionless with the sun at his back; got an immediate impression of cat-like stealth and menace as he let the doors slap to and approached the bar.

'The Last Water-hole,' he said, in a voice grating with thirst. 'Quite a name for a run-down saloon.'

Bobbie Lee looked at him. Saw a tall man, whip-thin, worn black hat with silver conchos sewn on the band, dark face white with dust; faded black clothing and a six-gun tied down on each lean thigh so his relaxed hands had no way of avoiding the walnut butts.

'What do you see up ahead?'

'The Staked Plains. A desert. Forty thousand square miles. No trees . . . nothing.'

Bobbie Lee nodded. 'So what's remarkable about the name?'

'For one thing,' the stranger said, 'that's not water you're drinking.'

And now Bobbie Lee grinned. 'Even the lizards pull a face at what passes for water in these parts.'

He slid down from the stool, walked around behind the bar, poured beer from a big jug and planted the glass before the lean man. It was picked up and drained at a single long draught. The man closed his eyes. Moisture from the drink had bitten into the dust around his lips. He wiped it with the back of his gloved hand, opened his eyes, took a deep breath and exhaled with satisfaction.

'I must have tasted better beer,' he said, 'but I really can't say when.'

'Any man settin' out across the plains,' Chip Morgan said, 'would be wise to stow that one in his memory so's he can dream about it in the days lying ahead.'

'Where I'm heading,' the man said, 'or if I'm heading nowhere at all, is none of your damn business.'

Yeah, Bobbie Lee thought, you're trouble all right – but if he wasn't heading anywhere, what kind of trouble could a man be planning in a settlement no better than a ghost town, on the edge of a landscape that was Hell on earth?

'I reckon,' Bobbie Lee said, 'old Chip was speaking hypothetically.'

The man's eyes – a washed out blue, Bobbie Lee noticed – settled on him like chips of ice.

'You sound like a man,' he said, 'who thinks too deep and uses words most people don't understand making comments that are just wasted breath.'

'Then let me waste some more,' Bobbie Lee said, and he reached beneath the bar, took hold of the big Greener shotgun and, without taking his eyes off the stranger, placed it on the bar. 'You don't look like a man about to set off across the Plains. I don't recall too many men stopping off here by the purest chance. That being so – and as the rooms I can offer ain't much different from that desert out there – I suggest you ride on to . . . wherever it is you're going.'

'About the only thing you got right about that,' the stranger said, 'is you wastin' your breath. You've done it again.'

'You're not welcome here,' Bobbie Lee said.

'Bein' welcome or not,' the other man said, 'has never been something that bothered me too much.'

'Maybe the saloons or towns where you ain't been welcome haven't pushed you hard enough,' Bobbie Lee said.

There was sudden movement and a light chuckle from the shadows at the end of the bar. A figure loomed. Eyes were bright and wide in a soft round face. A faint flush tinged the cheeks.

'Leave it, Jason,' Bobbie Lee said.

But the lad came forward. His tread was heavy. He was not a nimble youth. His innocent eyes were fixed on the stranger. One hand lifted. A finger pointed towards the door.

'You've got to go, mister,' he said – and again he chuckled with delight. 'My pa, he don't *like* you.'

'Maybe your pa should express his own opinions—'

But then the stranger abruptly broke off. Jason was still moving towards him. He was deceptively fast. His hand still pointed towards the door. But the other reached for the stranger. Jason stumbled close, clumsy, ungainly, but bearing down on the gunman with one playful aim in his simple mind. His big hand came up and clamped on the stranger's shoulder. He wrenched the man around, tried to swing him towards the door.

'Jason!' Bobbie Lee roared, and he started around the bar.

He forgot about the Greener.

Along the bar, Chip Morgan weighed up the situation. His eyes were narrowed. He came down weightily from the stool and lunged for the shot-gun.

The man with the pale eyes moved with lazy speed.

His wiry body was braced against young Jason's unnatural strength. He was still holding the empty glass. He let it fall. It hit the boards and shattered. With both hands free he went for his six-guns. The double draw was whisper smooth. His right hand was somewhat restricted, but he was unfazed. He brought the pistol up hard against young Jason's soft belly. Rammed the muzzled savagely into the mound of flesh. And he pulled the trigger.

In the same instant the six-gun in his left hand roared.

Bobbie Lee was still coming around the end of the bar. He heard the roar of one six-gun. The strangely muffled discharge of the second. He saw the Greener flipped away from Chip Morgan's desperately reaching hand as the hot lead rang against the barrel. Then Jason staggered back-wards towards him. Bobbie Lee reached out – too late. The boy's legs buckled. He flopped backwards to the floor. An arm was flung wide in the sawdust. His head rolled sideways. Already glazed, his eyes stared sightlessly towards the sunlight shafting through the door and sparkling on the shards of broken glass.

'If he was too simple to see danger here and now,' the stranger said with a terrible flat intonation, 'he had no chance of staying alive for the next couple of days.'

TWO

'I don't know what he meant,' Bobbie Lee said. 'I asked – and he laughed in my face.'

He was at the table in the kitchen at the back of The Last Water-hole. The uncurtained window looked out over the empty grassland. The sun had sunk behind the distant hills. Now the moon was floating, seeming to move lazily across a flamingo-pink evening sky washed with cool silver as high, drifting clouds crossed its face. Bobbie Lee could-n't see the square, but he knew that an oil lamp glowed on the general store's gallery. Chip Morgan was there, in the shadows, sharing a jug of whiskey with Will Blunt.

Will had stayed behind after the Halt's residents had turned out for Jason's burial. In the dusty cemetery the unshaven men had stood with their hats in their clasped hands and with heads bowed. The women had clustered in the shade of the lone cottonwood. For want of a clergyman it was Bobbie Lee who recited a simple prayer as the coffin was lowered.

He had been numb with shock, and conscious that every person there had seen Jason almost every day of his short life while he, Bobbie Lee, had been rampaging through the lawless West.

Cassie, too, had remained behind after the funeral, and with her question answered she was looking hard across the table at Bobbie Lee.

'He murdered your son – but still you gave him a room.'

'Look on it as a period of waitin' and watchin',' Bobbie Lee said. 'For some damn reason there's a couple of days to go to something we don't know about. There's a clock tickin' the time away, and we don't know why. But if that feller's stuck here in the Halt waitin' along with us, then he sure as hell ain't goin' nowhere.'

He always felt slightly uneasy in blonde Cassie's presence. He supposed it was embarrassment, but for the life of him he couldn't figure that out. He guessed she was pushing thirty. As he was thirty-six, they were roughly of an age. So why the discomfort?

She was watching him now, and despite the sympathy at his loss her face and her blue eyes couldn't entirely lose her habitual look of mild amusement. Bobbie Lee always got the impression she was secretly laughing at him and he couldn't figure out why.

'So he's here paying you rent for a room like a jail cell, and you're content to watch and wait?'

'That's about the size of it.' He grinned in the lamplight. 'And ain't that what we do most days

17

here in the Halt?'

'And you've got no ideas?'

'No more than you – unless you know something and ain't tellin'.'

'I know his type – but that's all.'

Did she, Bobbie Lee wondered? The stranger was a gunslinger. No damn doubt about that. But if Cassie was saying she recognized the type, well, that surely led to a whole lot of unanswered questions, and maybe explained her amusement.

She was pursing soft lips as he studied her face. 'One man. A gunslinger. On his own.' She thought for a moment. 'Nothing happens here in the Halt, Bobbie Lee. A man could set waiting for twelve long months, and he'd be a full year older but in no way any wiser.'

'So if there's nothing for him,' Bobbie Lee said, 'why's he come here, why's he waitin'?'

'And why did he gun down your son?'

Bobbie Lee slowly shook his head. There was a whiskey bottle on the table. An empty glass in front of him. He'd touched neither. A glass of water in front of Cassie was also untouched. Bobbie Lee poked a finger at his glass. Moved it around on the table. Pulled a face as he thought about that question.

Why? Why *would* a man walk in and gun down a helpless boy?

'He was making a point, stamping his authority,' he said softly. 'He walked in, and straight off he was the hard man. A fool could see that. But lookin' hard and actin' hard ain't the same as

18

slamming home the message in a way that hits folks smack beteen the eyes. Then Jason walked in and acted the way he always did – and the man had his excuse.'

'So now he's a man to be feared,' Cassie said, and nodded agreement. 'You're right, Bobbie Lee. You and Chip and my pa, after what he's done you'll all think twice about crossing him. And when you come up against a man like that, if you take the time to think twice – you're dead.'

'He's ridden in, and he's set the stage,' Bobbie Lee said, firm in that conviction but not entirely agreeing with Cassie. The days were long gone when he would think twice about crossing men like this stranger. Fifteen years ago, lacking in experience, well, maybe so. But now. . . .

'That's what he's done, he's set the stage,' Cassie said, as she rose to leave and reached across to touch Bobbie Lee's hand. 'Now all *we've* got to do is wait for curtain up and the show to commence.'

Later, lying under a single blanket on the cot in his room, Bobbie Lee thought about Jason, and mulled over the mysteries of life and death.

As a father, he supposed he should be experiencing grief at the boy's death, but all he could recognize was anger. That, he knew, was the emotion most men would feel at such a senseless killing. And because of the way things had turned out, he never had been much more than that to young Jason: just another man, another stranger who from time to time appeared out of nowhere and just as quickly rode away across the north Texas plains.

Sixteen years back, he'd been a young *married* man. But a difficult childbirth had snatched his wife from him and left him with a damaged son who never would put much distance between himself and childhood. That prospect was clear from the outset. For Bobbie Lee, it was too much to take. His wife had died. His son needed constant care. And so he left one-year-old Jason in the care of his grandmother, and spent the next fifteen years roaming the West pursued by an awful guilt that changed his character, turned him into a different man. A violent man. A man feared by all, but respected only by those outlaws who envied his prowess with a gun.

And then – then what? After fifteen years, what had gone wrong? Or, to put it in a more favourable light, what had gone right?

Bobbie Lee stirred uneasily on the hard mattress. He could hear the clink of bottle and glass through the thin wall, and knew that in the next room the stranger was lying awake. His kind would not be tormented by guilt. He would be looking back on a job well done; the first phase of a plan successfully accomplished; a base established in a small, cowed community on the edge of the Staked Plains.

But a base from which to launch – what?

What the hell, Bobbie Lee thought, is going on here?

Easier by far, he knew, to explain what had

happened twelve months ago to put an end to his own fifteen years of hell-raising. That was an easy one: his mother had died. A death had changed his life. Made everything right. Brought him home. Given him the ownership of the saloon once run by his father.

Left him, for twelve months, caring for a son he had never succeeded in knowing. Or, God help him, in loving.

Now he's gone, Bobbie Lee thought bitterly. And all he had left was the settlement of Beattie's Halt and an establishment called The Last Water-hole on the edge of a great white desert, and if the stranger who had ridden in was planning on taking any of that away from him, well, he could think again.

A death had brought Bobbie Lee home to a year of contentment. A senseless death had shattered that calm and taken away his only son. And if it took more deaths to restore order and enable Bobbie Lee to hang on to what he had left – and let his neighbours go on living the life they had chosen – well, fifteen years of riding the owlhoot would make him a very hard man to beat.

And, as he drifted into sleep, Bobbie Lee had a sneaking suspicion that blonde Cassie was already well aware of that fact.

THREE

Around about that same time, the stranger was lying back on his bed in the next room, hands clasped comfortably behind his head. He was somewhat muzzy-headed. The whiskey bottle stood empty on the table. He'd drunk it dry while listening idly to the murmur of conversation from downstairs without deciphering a single word; heard the girl leave, the rattle of hooves as she rode the short distance to her pa's farm; followed Bobbie Lee's footsteps in his mind as the man came upstairs, entered his room and shut the door.

He was reasonably happy, the stranger.

Hell, he had reason to be.

He had set out from the land on the southern reaches of the Nueces river with a purpose, with everything clear in his mind. Days later, within a few short hours of arriving in Beattie's Halt – a hamlet that just happened to be in the right place – he was some way towards achieving his aims.

Had the killing been necessary?

He supposed not. But the kid had annoyed him,

his skill with the six-guns in the gunbelt now hanging from the chair had made a big impression on the two men in the bar – and for some time he'd been operating on a short fuse. It was that same simmering anger that, a clear six months ago, had crystallized his intentions, turned those intentions into a viable plan and seen that plan evolve from a vague idea into a campaign that would see wrongs righted, see a powerful man pay for his sins.

The stranger chuckled in the darkness.

The beauty of it was, the powerful man was completely unaware of the blow that was about to fall. He had plans of his own, *big* plans, but those plans would fail, what he was setting out to do would come to naught – and all because the stranger had decided enough was enough.

The twelve months needed in the planning had passed quickly, but twelve months could never be considered a long time when compared with the time that had been stolen from the stranger when his life was torn apart, destroyed. That stolen time amounted to five years of back-breaking toil that had seen a dream realized. That dream had been shattered, taken from him by the powerful man who, in the space of a single year, spring to spring, had squeezed him dry.

So now it was fitting that the powerful man's life would also be destroyed in the space of twelve months. And that twelve months, the stranger thought with deep satisfaction, had but two short days to run.

In the darkness he rolled a cigarette. The match

flared. Smoke drifted. The cigarette's end glowed.

Tomorrow would see the arrival of the others. Strangers, three of them. Strangers who were costing him money. And again the stranger chuckled in the darkness. Costing *money*, yes, but the money could in no way be considered his. The money to pay for the necessary manpower and guns had come easy, because once the plan had begun to evolve, inhibitions had fallen by the wayside; the law had become an annoying hindrance to be brushed aside. If he was to succeed, the stranger had realized, the morals of the decent citizen had also to be cast by the wayside.

Now it was almost over.

In two days, the powerful man who had torn the stranger's dreams to shreds would meet his own, personal hell.

FOUR

Bobbie Lee was woken by the rumbling of the wagon that had arrived with supplies for Chip Morgan's general store. Dust drifted through the open window. He could hear the mules stamping and blowing, the laughter as the driver jumped down to josh with Chip, the lighter, feminine tones as Alice came out to offer the man hot coffee.

The room adjoining Bobbie Lee's was silent. As he rolled out of his blankets and pulled on pants and shirt, he caught the scent of frying ham. His jaw tightened. When he stamped downstairs he found the man with the two six-guns belted around his lean hips sitting at the table in the kitchen at the rear of the saloon. He was bent over, tucking into a plate heaped with ham and eggs. A coffee pot bubbled on the stove.

'Make yourself at home,' Bobbie Lee said.

'Yeah, well now, I sorta figured this place is café as well as water-hole, but I couldn't locate the help.'

'People hereabouts live at home, cook their own

breakfasts – work hard.'

'That puts me at a disadvantage.' The stranger looked up, grinned wolfishly. 'Work of any kind makes me a mite queasy. I'm in *your* home, and ten minutes ago you were snoring so mightily I thought I'd leave you be.'

Bobbie Lee was accustomed to preparing the food, and eating alone. A glance told him this man understood that, and had left everything close to the stove ready for his eventual appearance. But this morning Bobbie Lee's appetite was blunted. Maybe that was because of the gunslinger's disturbing presence. More likely, it was because he knew with deep sadness and regret that, when he *had* eaten, he would not be going to the stairs to call his son Jason down for his breakfast.

For that unexpected emptiness in his life, this man was entirely to blame.

'How long before you do that?' Bobbie Lee said.

'Leave you be for good?' The man shrugged. 'Let's call it a couple of days, then wait and see what happens.'

'Two days,' Bobbie Lee mused aloud. 'I can understand that, but this *wait and see what happens* has got me baffled. You awaitin' a message from the Lord?'

The man set aside his plate with a clatter, settled back, fixed a pensive gaze on Bobbie Lee.

'Some time today you'll be getting another three unwelcome guests.' He waited, saw Bobbie Lee's frown, lazily tugged the makings out of his vest pocket. 'The man wearing buckskins has got

26

some Irish in him. He's called Murphy. A second you'll remember by the big rifle he never lets out of his sight. That's Sangster. The third is called Cleet.' The stranger grinned at Bobbie Lee. 'You be very careful when that feller's around.'

'Sounds to me like you're movin' a whole damn army in here, piece by piece,' Bobbie Lee said, and saw the man's eyes narrow and harden. 'Maybe you'd best tell me your name before the war starts and you get yourself killed.'

The man blew a cloud of smoke from the freshly lit cigarette.

'Van Gelderen,' he said softly. His eyes were thoughtful. 'But what about you and that woman?'

'Cassie Blunt?'

'Yeah. I heard you two talking down here last night, for quite a while. You two real close? Maybe figurin' on getting hitched?'

The question took Bobby Lee by surprise, sent his thoughts flying wildly in directions he had never allowed himself to consider. For a few moments he was flustered as Van Gelderen watched him, his eyes strangely speculative. Then Bobby Lee shook his head.

'Leave Cassie well out of it—'

'Another thing I can't figure,' the man called Van Gelderen cut in. 'I rode in here, and before you even knew my name I'd pulled a gun and your boy's lyin' dead on the floor. Yet here you are, next morning, standing there large as life and talking to me as if I'm one of your best friends.'

'Hah!'

27

'Now if that was me,' Van Gelderen said, 'and it was my kid who'd been gunned down – I think I'd be doing something to put things right.' His pale eyes were watching Bobbie Lee. 'I mean, it's not as if you don't know the killer's name, where he's at; it's not as if you've got to make the effort to go looking for him an' all. . . .'

'You're absolutely right,' Bobbie Lee said, as he swung abruptly on his heel. 'You've got cronies coming to back up any play you make, Van Gelderen, but nothing can change the fact that you walked in here and shot dead a helpless young boy – my boy or someone else's son, that don't alter the facts. You pulled the trigger. That makes you a cold-blooded killer. I'd suggest instead of philosophizing, from now on you spend time watching your back.'

Bobbie Lee's head cleared as soon as he stepped down off the gallery into the morning sunlight and crossed the dusty square to the general store. The goods ordered by Chip Morgan had been off-loaded. There was no sign of the driver, but as Bobbie Lee ran up the steps he could hear the murmur of voices, the clatter of a cups.

The interior of the store was cool and dim, the air larded with the various aromas of the goods Chip Morgan offered for sale. Alice was behind the hardwood counter, her round face pink and cheerful. That cheerfulness changed to concern when she saw Bobbie Lee. Chip was off to one side, dressed as always in undershirt and work pants, sitting on newly arrived sacks of grain. The driver was holding a steaming cup.

Without preamble, Chip Morgan said, 'Where is the sonofabitch?'

'His name's Van Gelderen,' Bobbie Lee said as Alice tutted her disapproval of her husband's language. 'He's out of bed, in my kitchen eatin' my food, and I can expect three more of his kind before the day's out.'

The look of disgust on the driver's face told Bobbie Lee he would have spat if he hadn't been enjoying Chip's hospitality.

'Name rings a bell,' the driver said, in tones made gravelly by the black tobacco he chewed. 'Heard of a Van something or other, robbin' a bank down around Amarillo, not that long ago, either. Killed the town marshal. Gelderen could've been it.'

'Already know he's a killer,' Chip said.

'Chip, you leave that while Bobbie Lee's around,' Alice said softly.

'It's all right,' Bobbie Lee said. 'Jason's at peace, probably for the first time in his . . .' He broke off and spread his hands helplessly as he realized what he'd been about to say. Recovering, he went on, 'What we've got to figure out is what this Van Gelderen's up to, and why he needs another three men to do it.'

'There sure as hell ain't no bank here for him to bust into,' Chip said.

'Nothing within a hundred miles of here,' Alice said.

'Yet, accordin' to this Van Gelderen, before this day's done there'll be four of them here kickin' their heels.' Bobbie Lee looked around him for enlightenment, saw none, quietly accepted the cup of coffee Alice had slipped away to pour.

'Yeah, well, I'm off,' the driver said. 'I've a way to go, and I'll ask around. But you folks here know what it's like: no stage, no telegraph.' He shook his head in resignation. 'If I pick up word of trouble brewing it'll be history by the time I make my next round.'

And then he was gone, Chip coming off his grain sack to see him out then returning to the counter where Bobbie Lee was now eating a slice of hot, greasy ham clamped between two thick slices of bread.

Alice had disappeared out back to carry on with her chores. As the wagon rumbled away across the square, Bobbie Lee took his breakfast to the grain sack and sat down. Chip leaned against the counter and began packing a corn-cob pipe with dark tobacco. He looked pensively at Bobbie Lee.

'So let's add up what we've got that'd draw a bunch of gunslingers to Beattie's Halt,' he said. 'We've got a saloon selling strong liquor and weak beer, that ain't averse to letting rooms to gunsling-ing drifters. We've got a general store with a limited stock of basic goods to supply trappers and ranchers and horse traders who ride into town' – he chuckled at the grand title he'd bestowed on the Halt – 'when loneliness drives 'em crazy. There's Comanche out there on the Staked Plains.

And then there's Will Blunt's farm.'

'Nothing of any value,' Bobbie Lee said, 'and I'm including the saloon my pa built up from nothing and let slide into ruin when he got too old to care.'

For a few moments there was a silence as Chip Morgan puffed on his pipe. Bobbie Lee finished off his coffee and slabs of fresh bread, wiped his palms on the seat of his pants as he stood up and paced restlessly.

As far as he could see, they were out of ideas. They were the inhabitants of a remote settlement on the edge of the barren wilderness that was the Staked Plains. The nearest town was more than 100 miles off to the East, boasted a population of 250 and a town marshal who emerged from year-long torpor only when he was up for re-election. The county seat, with its sheriff, was even further away.

The wagon driver had emphasized their isola-tion: there was no stage, no telegraph. They were cut off from civilization, a dot in a wilderness bounded by the Cap Rock to the east, Mescalero Ridge to the west. The Llano Estacado was a daunt-ing barrier to the north.

Did that tell him something?

'You know, the only possible attraction Beattie's Halt could have,' Bobbie Lee said thoughtfully, 'is its lack of attraction.'

'I wondered when you'd figure that out,' said a tall, thin man who'd come in unnoticed out of the blazing morning sunlight to cast a long shadow in the doorway. 'Only possible reason outlaws'd make for a place like this is because it's a haven. The saloon's already been taken over. And they've established a powerful presence by murdering Bobbie Lee's boy.'

'I think Will's got a point,' Bobbie Lee said drily. 'And I reckon I know who gave him the idea.'

'Yeah, Cassie was working things out while she talked to you last night. And she always was the Blunt family's deep thinker,' Will Blunt said.

'Well, this ain't no fortress,' Chip Morgan said, 'but it sure as hell has its good points. A man can see for miles in most directions. Any posse heading this way'd have a hard time catching outlaws with their pants down.'

Blunt wandered across to the counter, plucked a stick of candy out of a jar and winked at Bobbie Lee.

He was as thin as a dry stick, Will Blunt and, like most of the inhabitants of Beattie's Halt, dressed for comfort in old work clothes. Thin greying hair drooped over a lined forehead. Deep set blue eyes peered out at the world with mild amusement, but there was an unmistakable hardness in the man.

Like all of us, Bobbie Lee thought, he's either a loser or a survivor – or both; has to be, to stay put in this Godforsaken spot. But that, Bobbie Lee knew, was now irrelevant. Yesterday a dangerous man had appeared out of the shimmering heat-haze, had committed a brutal murder, and now they were all threatened. Maybe life in the Halt was precariously balanced between indolence and the struggle to survive, but it was all they had and, within its limitations, they were comfortable.

But if they didn't act, and act fast, a lazy, aimless existence that had always seemed to stretch into eternity would be brought to an abrupt and violent end.

'He's out there,' Chip Morgan said, breaking into Bobbie Lee's thinking.

All three men hugged the store's deep shadows as they rushed to peer through the open door across the dusty expanse to The Last Water-hole.

Van Gelderen was on the gallery. The matched six-guns were deadly weapons of destruction on his lean thighs. Much as Bobbie Lee had done yesterday, he was up against the rail squinting into the distance.

Then, as they watched, he clattered down the steps and crossed to where his horse was dozing at the hitch rail. He squinted up at the blazing sun, then placed his hands flat on one of the bulging saddle-bags as if feeling the contents.

'What the hell's he playing at?' Bobbie Lee said.

'Maybe he figures the jerky he's got stowed in there will go bad in the heat.'

'Jerky breaks a man's teeth,' Blunt said, 'but I ain't never seen it go bad.'

Van Gelderen was now round the horse's other side, feeling the second bag. Then, with a shake of the head, he quickly unbuckled both bags, draped them over his shoulder and went back inside The Last Water-hole.

'Taking them to his room,' Blunt said.

But the little incident was over, and interest had faded.

'Bobbie Lee, you say three men are arriving some time today?' Chip Morgan said quietly.

Will Blunt knew nothing of this. He flashed Bobbie Lee a quick glance.

'Before nightfall,' Bobbie Lee said.

'Which could mean any time at all,' Blunt said.

'They get here,' Morgan said, 'it's over. Finished. We can maybe handle one man, but four hard-bitten characters with well-oiled six-guns. . . .' He shook his head.

'Between us,' Blunt said, 'we can do it, but we have to act now.'

Morgan stepped into the shaft of sunlight, then turned away and walked back into the store. His face betrayed grave misgivings.

'It's all come hammering out of the blue. Too fast for me. And it's a long time since I've seen my pistol, never mind pulled the trigger.'

'I'm willing to try,' Blunt said from the doorway, 'but the best I can do is an old percussion rifle coated with a couple of years' rust.' He looked across at Bobbie Lee who had followed Morgan, a question in his blue eyes.

'Van Gelderen's slug put paid to my shotgun,' Bobbie Lee said, and heard Blunt's exclamation of chagrin. Or maybe it was disbelief. 'I've got a gunbelt tucked away somewhere in my room. . . .'

'Damn right you have,' Blunt said, under his breath, as he gazed into the dazzling sunlight.

'The man's in your home, enjoying your hospitality, Bobbie Lee,' Chip Morgan said, his face alight with hope. 'He'll expect you to be there, so you get over there now. Go up and dig out that gunbelt. Buckle it on. Then you come walking down the stairs, and you shoot that murdering sonofabitch in the back.'

From behind the counter there was a gasp. Alice had emerged from the rear of the premises. She had her hand to her mouth. But despite her obvious shock at what she'd heard, her mild eyes were expressing a different sentiment. She was nodding as she gazed at Bobbie Lee.

And she had already placed a heavy Dragoon pistol on the counter.

Chip Morgan managed a sheepish grin.

'I guess it wasn't too far away after all,' he said. 'You get over there, Bobbie Lee. I'll give you a couple of minutes. Then I'll stick that big old shooting iron down the back of my pants, and wander over. If you don't get him from the back, I'll get him from the front.'

'Nobody's doing anything,' Will Blunt said from the doorway, 'because it's already too late. Three riders're coming in from the east right now. In ten minutes or so we'll be outnumbered and outgunned. You've got time to take Van Gelderen, but those riders'll blast us off the face of the earth.'

FIVE

It was decided that Will Blunt would head home to the farm and warn Cassie. Chip Morgan would go with Bobbie Lee the short distance across the square, the Dragoon pistol tucked in his waistband at the small of his back.

Alice would do nothing. The aim for all of them was to give the impression that life in Beattie's Halt was continuing as normal.

And doing nothing was pretty much all that ever went on in the Halt.

Blunt left the store by the back door. Bobbie Lee and Chip went out the front. From halfway across the square they could see the riders Blunt had spotted, still a mile away but clearly visible in the brilliant light, bright metal flashing in the sunlight, the horses trailing a plume of dust.

Van Gelderen had gone back into the saloon.

When Bobbie Lee led the way inside, the gunslinger was sitting at a table close to the window. He'd undoubtedly watched their approach. His eyes held a wicked glint.

'I guess you're feelin' pretty smug,' Bobbie Lee said.

'Satisfied,' Van Gelderen said. 'Everything's going according to plan.'

Chip had made his way behind the bar and was pouring himself a glass of beer. He raised the jug to Bobbie Lee, who shook his head as he climbed onto a bar stool.

'It's the plan that interests me,' Chip said, propping his elbows on the bar. 'You said something about a couple of days; we're well into the first: are we going to be told?'

'Told?' Van Gelderen smiled thinly. 'My plans are no concern of yours.'

'I'd say something that warrants the death of a young boy concerns all of us.'

Van Gelderen shrugged. 'That's in the past. The kid's dead. You draw your head in, there'll be no more trouble. Before you know it, we'll be out of here.'

Bobbie Lee and Chip exchanged glances.

Van Gelderen saw the look.

'I say something funny?'

'We had it figured different, that's all,' Bobbie Lee said.

'What figured – and different how?'

'We had you staying on. You and your cronies. Your *compadres*.' Bobbie Lee let that sink in then paused, treading carefully. 'Seems like you've made your point, staked a claim here. Why keep on riding when you've made yourself an alternative?'

He'd taken Van Gelderen by surprise. The surprise registered. Then the implications.

'You think I'm an outlaw? You think those men riding in are *outlaws?*'

'If you tell us we've got the wrong end of the stick,' Chip Morgan said, 'we'll apologize.' He took a slow drink, his eyes never leaving Van Gelderen.

'That's exactly what I'm saying: you're wrong.'

Bobbie Lee took a deep breath. His arm made a sweeping gesture.

'Two six-guns, tied down with rawhide thongs. Lightning fast, two-handed draw. A different target with each pistol.' He shook his head.

'Sounds to me,' Van Gelderen said, 'like you're talking from personal experience. I guess a saloonist sees all kinds, but that's not the way I'm reading it. Maybe you've spent time as a lawman. Or could it be that what you see in me is a reflection—'

He broke off as a rattle of hooves announced the arrival of the three horsemen. Clouds of dust drifted across the saloon's windows, obscuring the view across the sunlit square. Moments later the doors banged open and the newcomers clattered in.

Outlaws, Bobbie Lee thought, despite Van Gelderen's denial. Gunslingers every one of them. Expressionless eyes accustomed to taking in surroundings at one sweeping glance. Gloved hands never straying far from the butts of pistols carried in low-slung holsters.

All but one. The third man looked different. He wore a mountain-man's hat, a fringed buckskin jacket, soft Indian moccasins tied at the knees. On the face of it, the odd one out – until the gaze rose to meet his eyes, and then it was clear that there was no difference at all. This was another man out of the same mould, but made to look different. Bobbie Lee found himself wondering why.

He turned to the bar to face Chip Morgan as the newcomers joined Van Gelderen at his table and chairs scraped on the boards as they sat down. The fresh stink of dust and horses was in the saloon. The men spoke in low voices. There was some laughter, then one of them called for drinks and for the next few minutes Bobbie Lee was kept busy.

Back at the bar, he looked at Chip.

'Why the odd one out?'

Chip shook his head. 'Doesn't fit, does he.'

'But he's there, one of them, so there must be a reason.'

'There's a reason behind all of this, but so far we've not figured it out.'

'You believe Van Gelderen?'

'That they're not outlaws?' Again Chip shook his head. 'They're a bad bunch. Owlhoots. But it's Van Gelderen has me puzzled. Something about him, I don't know. Hard, yes, as hard as nails, but there's a lot of hard men out there and they ain't all bad. One possibility is he's hired these fellers to do a job, but then we're back where we started because he killed your boy and I'd say that makes him as bad as them.'

The low murmur of conversation washed over Bobbie Lee as he thought about that. He knew they'd figured wrong: Van Gelderen and the new arrivals were not in the Halt looking for a permanent outlaws' retreat. They had to think again, and Chip Morgan's fresh theory made a lot of sense. The trouble was, they were no better off. While mulling over possibilities they'd already established that there was nothing of worth within 100 miles of Beattie's Halt. So if these men *were* hired guns – then what was the job? What were they going to steal – because, in the end, didn't it always boil down to money.

'The odd one out's leaving,' Chip said quietly.

Bobbie Lee slid awkwardly down from the stool as if he had a crick in his back, stretched, turned to lean back against the bar and forced a wide yawn.

The man dressed in buckskins was already pushing through the door. He stopped on the gallery, donned his hat, stamped his moccasined feet and was gone. Hooves clattered as he departed in a hurry.

The outlaws had ridden in from the east. This man spurred his horse in a westerly direction. Bobbie Lee wondered about that. Wondered if, when the two days were up, Van Gelderen and the rest of them would also head west. That, too, would make sense, because if they were after rich pickings then much lay in that direction. But a hell of a long way in that direction – and it still didn't explain the stopover in the ghost town that was

Beattie's Halt. Nor did it explain why one man had ridden away, yet the others remained; why Van Gelderen had specified a two-day stop in Beattie's Halt.

Then, suddenly, Bobbie Lee became aware that a silence had fallen over the room.

Behind him, on the business side of the bar, Chip Morgan said tensely, 'Watch yourself, Bobbie Lee.'

'Don't I know you from somewhere?'

The man who had spoken was unshaven, heavy-set. His eyes were pale. He had left Van Gelderen and the other man at the table and moved to the centre of the room. Now he stood with legs braced in the centre of the sawdust-covered floor, hands loose close to his gun butts, those pale eyes fixed on Bobbie Lee.

'Somewhere's a big place,' Bobbie Lee said.

'How about Laredo? Tucson, maybe?' The man was prodding his own memory while his eyes drank in Bobbie Lee's appearance.

'Go back to your drink, give your mind a rest,' Bobbie Lee said, and he deliberately turned his back on the outlaw.

A big mistake.

'Godammit!' the man said. 'Knew of a feller used to do that. He'd get involved in an altercation. Turn his back like it was finished. Only it never was. . . .'

Slowly, Bobbie Lee again turned to face the man. And now he realized his mistake, and also knew that he had gravely erred by not going upstairs for his gunbelt.

'Anything else?'

The man's grin didn't reach his cold eyes.

'Knew his name.'

'Mine's Bobbie Lee.'

The man shook his head. 'That's not all of it.'

'It's enough.'

'Enough for a man who wants to hide. Only thing is, the initial letters're a giveaway. Because the feller who had a habit of turning his back before he drew his pistol and killed a man stone dead was B.L. Janson – the Caprock Kid.'

'You're dreaming—'

'Killed a friend of mine.'

'Not me.'

'Oh yes.' The man's eyes had narrowed. They swept over Bobbie Lee, took note of the slim hips, the absence of a weapon. 'Another trick the Caprock Kid had. He'd leave his gunbelt some-place. So it'd look like he was unarmed. Only—'

'I'm sorry about your friend,' Bobbie Lee said, and half turned, gesturing, anxious to put an end to the incident.

The gesture was another mistake.

The outlaw saw it. Misread Bobbie Lee's intentions. And went for his six-gun.

It cleared leather in a blur. The hammer snapped back. Then the pistol cracked.

Bobbie Lee was driven back by the bullet. It was as if he'd been hit by a battering ram. The blow to his chest slammed him back against the bar.

Through the singing in his ears he thought he heard Chip Morgan scream in anger. Then he slid down the bar into a bottomless pit of blackness and silence.

SIX

'If you're right, then my luck's in,' Van Gelderen said. 'I had my suspicions, thought I recognized him and so I tested him out with a few comments.' He shook his head. 'The man didn't blink, so maybe rumour is right and he's got no idea what happened that day.'

He was at a table talking to the man who had gunned down Bobbie Lee. With the buckskin-clad man riding hard to the west and the third newcomer over at the bar, they were alone.

'I am right,' the gunman said. 'The Caprock Kid. Had that trick of turning his back to put the other man off his guard. Or he'd leave his gunbelt off, rely on a hideaway tucked in his boot. Or in a holster back of his shoulder so's he could look like he was scratchin' his neck, make the draw. A single shot derringer was all he needed. . . .'

Van Gelderen nodded acceptance. He trusted this man. His name was Cleet. That's all he'd offered, and it was enough for Van Gelderen. He had gone to this man first, met him in a filthy *cantina* with broken shutters and a dirt floor, been served mescal by a one-eyed Mexican barman then asked Cleet to find him another three men. Hired guns. But there was a stipulation: one of those men had to be dressed in a certain way, and be capable of carrying off a deception.

'So now we wait, and we hope he lives, because now that I've found him I want him for myself,' Van Gelderen said. He let that sink in, then went on, 'The other man, the man we're here to stop – you see him on your travels?'

'Last I heard is we lost touch. But news travels slow.'

'Yeah, but is he heading this way?'

'This is his home. Why would a man pass up the opportunity of visiting his folks? Yeah, he's heading this way, and if he keeps on ridin' the way he was doin' he'll be here before sundown.'

'That's good,' Van Gelderen said.

Cleet grinned. 'You want me to remove him?'

'No. I want him brought down before he gets close to these peasants, these ignorant *campesinos*. I want him dead before he has the chance to open his mouth so wide he gives the game away.'

'That'll be a chore to Sangster's liking.' Cleet jerked his head at the man drinking at the bar. 'And after that, when this man's dead?'

'We're finished here. We ride west, offer our services. Or maybe we stay out of sight. Keep off the skyline. Watch and wait. Observe from a distance while Callaghan does what he's being paid to do.'

Callaghan. A killer dressed in worn buckskins. The man who was not what he seemed. The man who would, by his deception, deliver to Van Gelderen the big man who had destroyed his dreams.

But before that. . . .

'Is Sangster still nursing that big buffalo gun?'

'Always,' Cleet said, and grinned. 'If he had a wife, she'd sleep on the floor.'

'Tell him to get out back now. Find a clear view and a support for that long barrel – then set, wait and watch.

SEVEN

Bobbie Lee came awake to greenish sunlight. It shimmered like the yellow rays from an oil lantern seen by a man lying wide-eyed at the bottom of a weed-clogged water hole. He felt as if he was lying on soft, warm mud. His next conscious thought was that he had died and was lodged on a slippery shelf somewhere between Heaven and Hell. Then the notion of a water-hole snapped him into full wakefulness that brought with it recognition and true awareness of his situation: he was in bed, in his room above The Last Water-hole's bar.

After that it was easy. The soft mud was his corn-husk mattress. Someone had cut out most of the harsh sunlight by closing the pale green curtains – probably Cassie, who was sitting in the wooden chair by the bed. He tried to sit up and she placed her hand flat on his chest and effortlessly held him down. The light pressure caused an immediate bolt of red-hot pain.

'You took a slug in the shoulder,' she said as breath hissed through his clenched teeth. 'The man who pulled the trigger thinks we carried you up here to bleed to death. Boy, is he going to get a shock when you go striding down the stairs.'

'Is that going to happen?'

'It'd better. Without you, there's no purpose or direction in what they do.'

'They?'

'Chip, and my pa. They're concerned because you're their friend – but this is happening to *you*, Bobbie Lee. Your boy died. Your saloon's been taken over by a bunch of owlhoots and it's you lying gunshot and helpless.'

'I thought I was about to stride downstairs and frighten that gunman to death.'

'Yeah, well, we'll have to work that out.' She smiled grimly. 'The slug went straight on through. Chip sewed you up with a big needle from his store. You'll be weak, but able to get around. But what I'm saying is, if you give up, Chip and my pa will go about their business with their eyes turned the other way, fingers crossed, hoping those fellers with their fancy six-guns ride away just like they rode in.'

'They'll do that,' Bobbie Lee said, 'but not before they've finished what they set out to do.'

'Which is?'

He shrugged, and at once wished he hadn't as pain lanced down his arm so that his fingers folded into a tight fist.

But it was his left arm, and at that realization he felt the first resurgence of optimism.

'If we knew that,' he said, 'stopping them would be a lot easier.'

'Stopping them is never going to be easy.'

He lay without speaking for a moment, aware of his parched mouth, the weakness that was like a full-grown steer lying on his chest. He must have licked his lips. Cassie put her hand behind his head and fed him cool water from a tin cup.

'I can't lie here.'

'You run a saloon on the borders of Hell. Chip's down there serving drinks to killers. You want to take over?'

'Two days is all we've got, Cassie,' Bobbie Lee said. He levered himself onto an elbow and swung his legs off the cot. The room went black. He felt himself sway. He swallowed hard and squeezed his eyes shut. When he opened them the room tilted, then steadied. He took a deep breath, and grinned weakly.

'This time,' he said, 'I'm strapping on my pistol.'

She helped him to slip his shirt on over the heavy bandages, held his boots as he stepped into them. He struggled, and the sweat was cold on his brow. But when he buckled the gunbelt around his waist its weight announced the strength of the weapon it carried and he knew it was an equalizer.

'All right,' he said huskily. 'Let's go down and scare the hell out of those fellers.'

He was making his way unsteadily towards the door when the bellow of a big gun split the quiet and knocked him back on his heels.

Over at Will Blunt's farm the shot was heard as a distant boom that sent chickens fluttering across the yard. Beth Blunt was feeding them. She looked up as they flapped and cackled. Then the shot's detonation registered in her mind and she looked quickly towards the house.

Will was on his way out, his eyes fixed on the open land to the south.

'Saw a rider comin' in,' he said. 'Now all I see is a horse.'

'Oh, my Lord!' Beth whispered. 'What have they done now?' and she covered her mouth with a work-worn hand.

'I'll go see. You get inside out the way, keep your head down.'

Blunt's skinny blue roan was saddled. He swung aboard, used the loose ends of the reins to whip it into a gallop and cut through a gap in his unfinished fence. The horse he'd spotted was standing lathered and head-hung some 400 yards away, its outline shimmering in the heat haze. Will covered the distance from farm to horse at a dead run. Before he was even halfway there he could see the dark shape lying crumpled in the clumps of dry grass.

As he drew close the waiting horse lifted its head. Blunt saw its nostrils flare. It backed away uneasily, showing the whites of its eyes.

Already got the smell of death in his nostrils, Blunt thought, and his jaw tightened as he slid the roan to a halt and swung down.

His arrival had brought a fresh swirl of dust that drifted across the fallen man. Blunt coughed, spat, then dropped to his knees.

'Easy, boy,' he said softly, absently, as the man's horse snorted nervously. But already Blunt was reaching out to grasp the fallen rider's shoulder. The man was face down. Blunt noted the faded buckskins. He frowned as instinct told him something was terribly wrong. Then he heaved the man over onto his back and horror knocked him back on his heels.

There was a single black hole in the front of the fringed jacket. No blood. The man had died instantly. But Will Blunt was no stranger to violent death. The horror had hit him hard and knocked him sick because when he turned the man over he had at once recognized the young face, the sightless grey eyes, and he knew he was faced with a chore no man alive could look forward to without trepidation and despair.

Bobbie Lee was making his slow way across the square to Chip Morgan's store when the sound of hooves reached his ears and he glanced away to his right to see Will Blunt spurring his horse through his broken-down fence and out across the open land to the south. Then the parched timber structure of The Last Water-hole got in the way and nothing could be seen of Blunt but the settling trail of dust.

Chip Morgan was out on his gallery, smoke curling from his corn cob pipe. He'd left the bar to look after itself when Van Gelderen slapped a handful of coins on the bar. There had been no need to count the money as he scooped it noisily into the tin box. Chip had seen at a glance that there was enough cash to pay for more beer than twice as many men could drink in a single afternoon.

'What the hell are you doing out of bed?'

'It was my intention to give those fellers a fright, show them a dead man up and walking,' Bobbie Lee said. He leaned against the hitch rail. His left arm was supported by a sling, the bandage a dazzling white in the sunlight. 'But I guess they've brushed all thoughts of me aside like a heap of useless trash and moved on. What d'you suppose that shot means?'

'Seems to me a feller like the Caprock Kid,' Morgan said with a speculative glance at his friend, 'would already have the answer figured out.'

'You're wasting time ruminating on the past when we're facing big problems here and now, Chip.'

'But that gunslinger was right about you. Hell, your name's there for all to see: B.L. Janson, but here in the Halt you've always been Bobbie Lee and I never put two and two together to get the right answer.'

'You saw what happened in there. The man he was facing was unarmed because he'd put a name and a reputation behind him. In twelve months that former self has already become a faint shadow. I'd like to think the shadow died when that shot was fired and what's left now is a man who's older, humbler—'

'And more peaceable – but still sensible enough

to strap on a well-used six-gun when circumstances call for it.'

'Put it any way you like, but for now put it behind you, because it sounds like Will's on his way back.'

Despite the talk, Bobbie Lee's mind and senses had been only half with Chip Morgan as he climbed the steps to the general store's gallery. In his memory he was still listening to the echoes of a shot that, for some reason he couldn't explain, had chilled him to the bone. Now the rattle of approaching hooves told him that Blunt – still out of sight – was heading back into the Halt. But because of his experience the sounds told him more than that. They told him that Blunt had ridden out alone and was coming back with a second horse. They told him that second horse was stepping nervously, erratically, backing off then abruptly picking up the pace. And when Blunt came around The Last Water-hole and started across the empty square, the reason for that second horse's fright and its curious gait became clear to both of the watching men. Will Blunt was leading the horse on a short rope tied to his saddle-horn. Across that second horse's saddle a dead man was draped face down and slack.

'Buckskins,' Chip Morgan said, as the two riders, one alive, the other dead, drew near. 'Wasn't that what that feller who rode out was wearing?'

'Yeah,' Bobbie Lee said. 'But why would they kill one of their own?'

Then Will Blunt was across the square and drawing to a halt in front of the store. He swung down from his horse, loose-tied the reins to the rail as the second horse backed and jerked its head against the tight rope, and came up the steps. His blue eyes were troubled. He looked beyond the two waiting men to the store's open door, saw Alice Morgan at the counter back in the shadows. Then his gaze fixed on Chip Morgan.

'Chip,' he said softly, 'there ain't no easy way to say this, so I'll say it fast before Alice comes out and hears what's goin' on. That man lyin' over the horse I brung in is your boy, Ed. He got took by that single shot. He must've been dead when he hit the ground.'

EIGHT

By late evening there was an air of disbelief hanging over Beattie's Halt. Twelve months ago, Bobbie Lee's mother had been a tired old woman and her death had come as no surprise, but in the space of two days the citizens of the Halt had found themselves gathering at the cemetery to bid farewell to a simple, innocent boy shot down at close range in The Last Water-hole, and a strapping youngster who had ridden in out of the blistering heat to be blown out of the saddle by a bullet from a powerful buffalo gun.

For the men of the Halt, that disbelief was larded heavily with loathsome feelings of guilt. The man called Van Gelderen had murdered Bobbie Lee's son and – of this Bobbie Lee had no doubt – had ordered the killing of Ed Morgan. Yet it had surely been within the power of Bobbie Lee, Chip Morgan and Will Blunt to avert the second of those deaths.

Jason had died as the direct result of a gunman's skill with a deadly weapon. Two pistols had been drawn. The gunman's left and right hands had been a blur, the killing had happened in the blink of an eye. Onlookers had been caught cold, but they were experienced men and should have learned from the boy's death. It was a warning, a harbinger of what would almost certainly follow, yet they had done nothing but offer to the killer the hospitality that was in their nature. Bobbie Lee had given Van Gelderen a room in The Last Water-hole, and sat with him at breakfast. He had stood by with scarcely a protest when three more men rode in. And Chip Morgan had served them all drinks; had been serving drinks to Ed Morgan's killer as Van Gelderen and the man called Cleet sat at a table planning the murder.

So it was with feelings of bitter regret that Bobbie Lee stood back from the small cluster of mourners gathered at Ed Morgan's fresh grave. But that regret was steadily being swamped by anger and a fierce determination. Cynics would say that he was experiencing a decent man's natural reactions that had come much too late, but Bobbie Lee knew full well that while it would always be too late to breathe life back into the dead men, it would never be too late to go after their killers.

Even as that growing resolve to see justice done was being strengthened by the sad sound of Will Blunt murmuring a final farewell at the edge of his son's grave, Bobbie Lee's attention was caught by the rattle of hooves. And when he turned to look down the slight incline from the cemetery to The Last Water-hole, it was to see three riders cantering without haste out of Beattie's Halt in the pale light of a rising moon: Van Gelderen, Cleet, and Ed Morgan's killer. The two days were up. The three killers were leaving town.

They were heading west, in the wake of their buckskin-clad compadre. If two deaths were to be avenged, Bobbie Lee knew he must follow the three riders.

But first there was some hard thinking to be done.

What better place to meet than in the familiar bar room at The Last Water-hole?

If the ghostly memories of gunsmoke lingered there, and in the moonlit open area out back where Van Gelderen's man had hunkered patiently to gun down Ed Morgan, then that was fitting. They were meeting to discuss what they should do about the men who had ridden in from the desert, killed two of their loved ones, and moved on as if they had done nothing worse than squash a couple of flies. And if the women of the Halt – Alice Morgan, Beth and Cassie Blunt – found themselves in an environment from which they were traditionally barred (though not as strictly as they might have been in a town of more importance, or temperance), they could console themselves with the knowledge that they were there to help right terrible wrongs and their opinions and suggestions would be welcomed.

'First off is that same vexing question,' Bobbie Lee said, looking at those gathered around the table. 'What the hell has been goin' on, what is still goin' on – if you ladies will excuse my profanity.'

'The real profanity is what's been done to this town,' Chip Morgan said, puffing at his corn cob. 'As far as I'm concerned you can swear your damn fool head off provided it gets us somewheres, and gets us there fast.'

All three women nodded agreement. Alice Morgan was red-eyed from weeping, and sitting close to Chip. Beth Blunt appeared to be in shock. Cassie was composed and thoughtful and seemed to be in tune with her pa, who was also doing some deep thinking. Looking at Ed Morgan's bereaved parents, Bobbie Lee had already decided that he would be relying on Will Blunt when the time came to go after the killers. Chip would have been his second choice for a companion at the best of times, but not now, with Alice so clearly in need of comfort and the presence of her husband.

'What's going on,' Cassie Blunt said, cutting into his thoughts, 'is those three men who rode into the Halt have got business somewhere to the west of here. Could be as far away as El Paso. Could be no more than ten miles down the trail. But that business is connected to or dependent on a man wearing buckskins' – and here she looked with sympathy at the Morgans. 'That's what Ed was wearing when he got killed, and that's what that nameless outlaw was wearing when he rode out.'

'If you're right, they knew Ed was coming,' Chip Morgan said bitterly. 'Seems like the only reason they rode in here was to kill my boy and replace him with one of their own.'

'Why?' Bobbie Lee said. 'What was so special' – and now it was his turn to look apologetic – 'about Ed?'

'Stop pussyfooting around,' Alice Morgan said. 'Nothing's going to get solved if you all back off every time Ed's name's mentioned.' She sniffed and dabbed her eyes with a 'kerchief. Chip fumbled for her hand on the table and gave it a squeeze. 'For what it's worth,' Alice said, 'I'll tell you two things special about Ed: he knew cattle, and he knew this area.'

'All right.' Bobbie Lee nodded. 'I don't know if that tells us anything or nothing, but it's given us something to work on. Any thoughts, Will?'

'Only one,' Will Blunt said, his eyes glinting. 'Charlie Goodnight.'

For a moment there was silence. Bobbie Lee knew Will's reference to Charlie Goodnight meant he was seeing links between the knowledgeable Ed Morgan's ride to Beattie's Halt, and the Goodnight-Loving cattle trail. In 1866, ranchers Charles Goodnight and Oliver Loving had blazed a trail from Texas through New Mexico with the aim of reaching the Colorado country. They hit trouble in an eighty-mile dry region that drove the cattle mad with thirst and halted the drive. Goodnight received compensation from government agents on a Navajo reservation who paid gold for the steers, and he returned home with the cash. Loving pushed on northward to Denver in Colorado with the cows and calves, but later died from an infected Indian arrow wound.

That had been but a few years ago, and it was that eighty-mile stretch of parched land that interested Bobbie Lee: part of the Llano Estacado, the Staked Plains. If there was a rancher out there planning on using the same route to drive his cattle northward to Colorado. . . .

Bobbie Lee looked at Alice Morgan, saw her nod, and pursed his lips.

'Yeah,' Bobbie Lee said softly, 'I reckon if a rancher brought his herd up the Goodnight-Loving trail and wanted to take it all the way across the Staked Plains, Ed would make as good a guide as any.'

'So why kill Ed?'

Bobbie Lee looked at Chip, chewed his lip while he did some more thinking, then said, 'A good guide was replaced by a bad one because someone somewhere is bearin' a grudge.'

'Name names, Bobbie Lee,' Will Blunt said.

'Why? You saw the man. If you want a name, try Van Gelderen.'

'You know him?'

'Not before the last two days. But he's the clear leader, mean as a sick rattlesnake, so, yes, I'd say it's him got it in for this rancher.'

'What about the man who plugged you?'

'Nope, never set eyes on him – though I'll admit I've had enough *mal hombres* in my sights to have forgotten a good half of them.'

'All right,' Chip said, 'so we agree on Van Gelderen. But what about the rancher? The grudge. Aren't we shootin' in the dark?'

'For Christ's sake,' Morgan said impatiently. 'This is not about Bobbie Lee, and it's not about some rancher and a big herd you fellers have plucked out of your imagination. Pure and simple, this is about a gunslinger called Van Gelderen who killed Bobbie Lee's son, another who used a long rifle to knock my boy out of the saddle.'

'And a third man who damn near killed me,' Bobbie Lee said softly as he gently massaged his shoulder through the white sling.

He knew they were wasting time talking when killers were eating up the ground to the west, putting miles between them and possible pursuit. But he was also pretty sure Will Blunt had got it right about the Goodnight-Loving trail, and with that accepted, everything fell into place. Van Gelderen ordered the killing of Ed Morgan, and replaced him with one of his own men dressed in identical clothes. That was no coincidence. There was a big herd out there. The owner would soon be pointing the lead steer towards the Staked Plains, and he would be putting his trust in an impostor, a man who would guide him not to prosperity, but to ruin. Somewhere along the line, the rancher – whoever he was – had crossed Van Gelderen. For that mistake, he would see his herd perish.

But then again, Bobbie Lee thought, so what? What did that – if it were true – have to do with anyone at Beattie's Halt? Sure, another man's misfortune was regrettable and should be prevented if at all possible, but truth was he could think all night, add what he knew to what he surmised and still arrive at the same inevitable conclusion: Chip Morgan was talking plain common sense. This was not about ranchers who could be figments of lively imaginations, nor of herds of ghostly steers being led blind into a searing wilderness. It was about two murders, and the outlaws who had committed those terrible crimes.

'All right,' Bobbie Lee said at last. 'Let's quit talking, saddle up and hit the trail.'

It sounded simple enough, but the population of Beattie's Halt comprised three men and three women and only one of the six could be described as young. Common sense told Bobbie Lee he was ruled out of the chase because of the fresh bullet wound in his shoulder. But he'd already admitted that eliminating himself from the males left Chip Morgan – a grieving father armed with a Dragoon pistol that'd take most of his strength to hold steady – and Will Blunt and his percussion rifle that was so rusty it would probably blow to pieces in his gnarled hands.

After his call for action, Bobbie Lee put those thoughts to the group gathered in The Last Water-hole's lamplit room and met with stiff opposition. Both Morgan and Blunt insisted Bobbie Lee should ride with them because of his experience on the wrong side of the law – that last endorsement given bluntly by Will Blunt who, it appeared, had always known more about Bobbie Lee's darker side than he'd let on.

But it was the 'ride with them' that was troubling Bobbie Lee: the wide gunfighting experience he was blessed with – poor choice of word, he thought wryly – had already warned him that Chip Morgan should remain behind, and the shortage of reliable weapons suggested Will Blunt might also be a liability.

The matter was in part settled by Cassie Blunt.

'Pa's rifle's in fine working order,' she said, when Bobbie Lee voiced his concerns. 'He doesn't know it, but every time I clean and oil my Henry I do the same to his old Sharps.'

Blunt blinked and widened his eyes at his daughter's words. 'You telling me you've got one of them .44 Henry rifles?'

'Ed Morgan got it for me, years ago, at my request. Got it engraved, too, with both our names.' She smiled with sadness at Chip Morgan. 'Just goes to show parents don't know everything their kids get up to.'

'All right,' Bobbie Lee said, 'that settles the question of fire power. Will, you ride with me. Chip, I'd like for you to stay here and run the bar, be hospitable to any visitors to The Last Water-hole.'

'Why me? Alice or Beth could handle that chore real easy.'

'The womenfolk are my reason for wanting you here: you'll be available to look after them if there's trouble.'

Chip still objected heatedly. 'You just heard Cassie. Will's gal's got herself a .44 Henry—'

'Yes,' Cassie cut in, 'but I'm riding with Bobbie Lee.'

The room went silent.

Bobbie Lee shook his head.

'Those fellers're too dangerous.'

'If two of you ride, you'll be outnumbered – maybe by more than you anticipate. You've got a bad shoulder, a six-gun you can shoot with one hand. Pa's got a single-shot Sharps. With me along the odds look better and, like Chip said, the gal's got herself a Henry repeater.'

She smiled sweetly.

'Give the repeater to your pa,' Bobbie Lee said, meeting her gaze.

'I could shoot the eye out of a crow while my pa's still looking for the goddamn bird,' Cassie said, and winked at her mother.

Will Blunt caught the look. He chuckled. 'I can't argue with that.'

Bobbie Lee thought for one swift moment, realized Cassie was right, and let his breath out in relief.

'So everything's settled? We're all agreed?'

'I guess so,' Chip Morgan said, still contriving to look disgruntled but obviously relieved to be staying home with his grieving wife while being of use.

Will Blunt was looking in some amazement at his daughter.

'Give us a half-hour,' he said, getting up from the table. 'We'll go get those weapons Cassie's been nurturing, pack supplies in saddle-bags, be back here ready to ride.'

'Bring extra water bottles,' Bobbie Lee said. 'The weather's going to get warm.'

And so the three Blunts left for the short walk over to their property where the windmill creaked in the mild night breeze, Chip and Alice Morgan taking the even shorter walk across the square to where the light glowed yellow in the window of their general store.

Bobbie Lee watched them from the gallery. Bathed in wan moonlight that picked out the ruts and undulations in the dusty old square he recalled with sadness that he had stood in that same spot when the sun had been beating down from a clear blue sky and, behind him, his son had been happily splashing soapy water onto the boards.

Two days ago. Now Jason was gone, one of Chip Morgan's sons had taken a bullet in the chest and was six feet under, and there was work to be done; the kind of work Bobbie Lee thought he'd left behind twelve months ago when he'd said goodbye to the owlhoot trail and ridden home to take over the family-run saloon on the edge of the Staked Plains.

He reflected on that for a few moments, his head growing dizzy with thoughts that were at best uncomfortable, at worst verging on the morbid.

Then he sighed, turned away from the rail and walked in to the echoing silence of The Last Water-hole.

PART TWO

THE MANHUNT

PART TWO

THE MANCHU

NINE

They made a strange, mismatched group, the members of that small, private posse: Bobbie Lee on his big sorrel mare riding awkwardly as he favoured his bandaged left shoulder, six-gun butt-forward in the holster on his left hip for an easy cross draw; Will Blunt on the skinny blue roan, the old but well-oiled single-shot Sharps jutting from the leather boot beneath his right knee; and his daughter, flaxen-haired Cassie, a small woman made to look larger than life as she rode behind the two men on her lively paint pony.

They rode out in clear moonlight, watched by a sombre, silent trio on the gallery of Bobbie Lee's Last Water-hole saloon. Behind the riders the lamps of Beattie's Halt were few, but warm and seductive nonetheless for ahead of them lay naked uncertainty. They had witnessed murder, and were hunting cold-blooded killers. But those killers could be lying in wait for them and so, as the warm lamplight of the Halt was washed away by the cold light of the moon, it was Bobbie Lee who took the lead after telling Will Blunt to fall back a full thirty yards, Cassie to put that same distance between her and her father and watch their back trail.

For if Van Gelderen was planning an ambush, he would be sure to let them ride past one man before giving the signal to open fire.

That the distance between them made for solitary riding was unavoidable. Bobbie Lee knew the dangers of bunching. A volley of rifle fire could wipe out men riding too close together. But he also knew that the disadvantages of riding alone could be outweighed by the consequent sense of responsibility; men forced to rely on their own ability to stay alive were unlikely to doze in the saddle.

And that, Bobbie Lee thought with a secret smile, applied equally to women – and yet again he found himself marvelling at the outstanding qualities of the young woman who, in trail drive terms, was now riding drag.

That thought at once took him back to the discussion in The Last Water-hole. He found himself wondering how close any of them had been to the truth when raising the possibility of a Texas herd out there, waiting to be guided across the arid Staked Plains.

Chip Morgan had pointed out the uselessness of conjecture when there were killers at large, deaths to be avenged, and Bobbie Lee had accepted those sentiments. But now, riding through the night with the only sounds the jingle of bits, the creak of leather and the soft snorting of the horses, he knew that what lay ahead needed his serious consideration. He needed his wits about him; to be forewarned was to be forearmed. As he rode, he was alert not only to the possibility of ambush – though for the life of him he couldn't see how such action would benefit Van Gelderen – but to what the night was telling him. He was looking ahead for the reflected glow of camp-fires; sniffing the air to detect their smoke, or the aromas of cooking food from a trail-drive chuck-wagon; listening hard for the faint but unmistakable murmuring that would indicate the presence in the vicinity of a large herd of cattle.

Will Blunt caught the sounds first.

'Cattle some way ahead.'

Cassie kicked the paint up to join him.

'If they're about to cross the Plains, night's the time to get started.'

By now they had both pushed up the trail to join Bobbie Lee, and all three were riding stirrup-to-stirrup.

'A good guide would know that,' Bobbie Lee said. 'But Van Gelderen's man might not have that wisdom.'

'They'll have it all figured out, one way or another, with cruel logic,' Will said. 'If we're thinking along the right lines, Van Gelderen wants to ruin a certain rancher. Best way of doing that in this situation is to put a big herd of cattle in the middle of the Staked Plains when the sun comes up.'

Bobbie Lee nodded. 'The rancher's heading for Colorado. He'll expect the guide to get him there,

71

maybe with a depleted herd but with plenty left to make him a big profit. I reckon you're right. Van Gelderen's man will play out his role, but at some stage arrange it so those steers are scattered to hell and gone.'

'One man?'

Bobbie Lee looked at Blunt and shook his head. 'The guide, plus Van Gelderen, Cleet, and the feller who shot Ed. More than enough if they work it right.'

For a while they rode in silence, listening for the faint, distant cries of 'punchers as they got a big herd up and moving. No such sounds reached their ears, but already they could detect the smell of cattle and dust carried on the night air, the smoke of the camp-fires.

'There's one thing wrong with that last supposition,' Bobbie Lee said at last. 'If Van Gelderen's hell-bent on revenge, he'll be forced to stay well clear.'

Cassie was quick to catch on. 'Sure. If there's been a feud between those two in the recent past, the rancher will know him by sight. I can see Van Gelderen stepping forward later, so he can have the satisfaction of knowing he's done his job and the rancher's staring ruin in the face.' She laughed softly. 'But will you listen to us, Bobbie Lee! Ranchers and herds, revenge and ruination. You realize all this is like Chip said, vivid imagination allowed to run riot?'

'There's a herd out there, so that's one thing we got right,' her father said. 'All we can do is press on, and see if the rest of the plot matches what we've dreamed up.'

'Yes indeed,' Bobbie Lee said. 'But I've got a horrible suspicion Van Gelderen knows I'm coming after him, and I'm bettin' he's got a couple more nasty tricks up his sleeve.'

The chuck wagon was canted at an angle on the side of the slope. It had been driven in fast with pots and pans clattering, and sited in a hurry so the cook could build his fire in its lee and get the Dutch oven settled on the hot coals before the herd arrived. That had happened at dusk, the full straggling column taking more than an hour to be swung around in a wide sweep by the point riders, worked close to the Pecos where steers, cows and calves drank their fill of the muddy waters before settling for the night.

Only then could the hands slide wearily from their saddles close to the chuck-wagon and set to work on the cook's interesting variation of Sonofabitch Stew, handed to them steaming on battered tin plates. Several had then ridden out to relieve those riding lazily on the flanks of the rest-ing herd, softly crooning Texas lullabies to soothe the animals while turning impatient eyes towards the sparks drifting skywards from the glow of the cook's fire.

The latecomers had now eaten, and all but the night guards circling the herd had turned in. Blanket rolls had been dragged from the chuck wagon's bed. Sleeping figures were shapeless heaps lying in the dappled shadows under the trees, alongside them the odd, angular shapes of boots and saddles. Smoke from the fires drifted pungently to mingle with the mist hanging low over the Pecos. A cowboy laughed at something another man had said. Nearby under the trees another sat cross-legged and held his hands to his mouth to cup the plaintive wailing of his mouth organ.

'What was that name again?'

Harlan Gibb looked up at the lean man with the badge pinned to his vest who had just ridden in, at the other rider with his hand on the stock of the long rifle jutting from his saddle boot and his horse positioned a few yards behind the lawman.

'B.L. Janson,' Cleet said. 'Bobbie Lee. You probably know him better as the Caprock Kid.'

'Do I?'

'Should do. He raised hell around your neck of the woods. South Texas. The gulf coast. Faded away about a year ago. If I were you, with that feller on the prowl I'd be worried about my herd.'

'But you're not me, Marshal. . . ?'

'Earp.' Cleet grinned. 'Pure coincidence. I'm no relation to that feller who bested Ben Thompson up in Ellsworth.'

Gibb nodded slowly, chewing on the information, frowning slightly as he let the fragments float around to form some sort of sensible shape in his mind.

'We've come halfway across Texas, pushed this herd through flooded river crossings, rescued cows and calves from sinkholes, rounded up the whole two thousand head after thunder caused 'em to stampede. Despite all those troubles, we've lost fewer than a dozen head.' He squinted at Cleet. 'You mind explainin' why a tired old outlaw should cause me a single moment's concern?'

'Tired and getting old he may be, but Janson's wounded and dangerous. You mentioned sinkholes. I was forced to pull my pistol on the Caprock Kid in a sinkhole by the name of Beattie's Halt. Plugged him in the shoulder. While there, I also picked up on some gossip. Lord knows why, but this man bears you a grudge. And he's doubly dangerous, because he's not operating alone. He knows you're here, knows you're taking a herd across the Staked Plains.'

'That's a long speech, Marshal Earp.'

'The next bit's short. You need an escort. Me and my deputy, Sangster—'

'I don't see the shine of a deputy's badge.'

Cleet shrugged. 'What you do see is a buffalo gun and a man who can shoot the black centre out of the Ace of Spades at any distance you care to name.'

'Maybe.' Gibb smiled, then shrugged. 'What you do is up to you. I've told you you're not needed, but I can't stop you riding into that baking wilderness if that's what you want.'

Cleet looked towards the trees, thinking of the timing.

'Your men are sleeping.'

'So are the cattle. You got here too early. We rest

75

all day tomorrow, move out at sundown.'

'You following the advice of your guide?'

Gibb pushed his lips out, his eyes narrowed, and Cleet grinned.

'Ain't no secret, no mystery. Ed Morgan rides herd down in Texas, but the reason he can take you across the Llano Estacado is because he was born in Beattie's Halt. You know Ed, so you already know that, an' me knowing Ed explains my presence here: I saw him in the Halt. We were sharing drinks when I was forced to plug the Kid. Ed told me what he was about to do, how you'd hired him. . . .'

Cleet shrugged, waited.

'Do I see more coincidence at work here? You ride into this Beattie's Halt, by chance run into Ed Morgan and the Caprock Kid—'

'The Kid runs the saloon. The Last Water-hole.'

The name brought a smile to Gibb's face. He hesitated, then shook his head. 'Suit yourself, Marshal.' He turned away. 'You and your deputy can bed down under the trees. Tomorrow's going to be a long day doing nothing. Use it to see the setup here, understand how we can handle anything this Caprock Kid throws our way – maybe change your mind about actin' as unpaid unwanted escorts.'

'If you've got doubts, sir, Ed Morgan will vouch for me.'

'I'm sure he will, but I look at a man and make my own assessment of his character.'

'Yeah,' Cleet said softly as Harlan Gibb walked

away, 'and men like you, they're so damn full of themselves they can't see it when they're busy diggin' their own graves.'

'Like you told him,' Sangster said laconically, 'we're only here to help.'

TEN

Bobby Lee and Will Blunt left Cassie tucked back in a thick stand of trees and pushed on through the night to locate the herd. She was out of sight, comfortable in a clearing small enough to be untouched by moonlight, her bedding unrolled and the Henry fully loaded and by her side.

Will had understandable misgivings at leaving her. She brushed them aside. The clearing was a natural fort, a hollow surrounded by stony banks. To get close without being seen, Cassie said, a man would be forced to come on foot through the woods. Only an Indian could do that in silence.

The two men covered a mile, then another, sensed in their bones they were getting close but still had no idea how they were going to handle the meeting with the rancher – if he existed; if he was about to take his stock across the Staked Plains; if Van Gelderen's man in buckskins was there with him – just too *many* ifs for Bobby Lee.

'But does it matter?' he said to Will Blunt. 'We're hunting a couple of killers. We'll get them, one way or another, whether they're heading north to Colorado or south through Texas.'

'Quit speculating,' Blunt said. 'Van Gelderen could be watching you right now, but you're out of time. We're so close the stink of the herd's taking my breath away.'

The trail was wide. They rode up a gentle grassy slope, thudded over the crest. Bobby Lee could see the lights of the camp-fires, beyond their flickering the gleam of the mist-shrouded Pecos River. The herd was a dark mass covering the ground like a monstrous swarm of bees. Now and then horns gleamed bone-white in the moonlight as a steer turned its head. Bobby Lee sniffed, caught the whiff of some kind of stew that set his mouth watering and his eyes hunting for the chuck-wagon.

'No guards.'

Bobby Lee grunted. 'Only the nighthawks. I can hear one of them crooning to those critters. This herd's not moving tonight.'

'Someone talkin' over that way.'

They swung right and down the slope, and now the smell of food was stronger and Bobby Lee knew the men who were too restless to sleep, or about to spell those watching the herd, were gathered in the warmth of the cook's fire.

As they rode down he could see the remuda in a simple rope enclosure, the horses dozing hip-shot; the pale bulk of the chuck wagon's canvas;

the dark shapes of men sleeping under the trees.

Then a tall figure was on its feet and moving away from the hanging lantern and the fire's glow to meet them. The long shadow falling across the grass faded as the man stepped out into the moonlight. Bobby Lee hissed a warning to Blunt and lifted the reins high to make his hands clearly visible.

'That's far enough, Janson.'

'Jesus!' Will Blunt said softly.

And over by the fire there was the ugly sound of a weapon cocking.

'What kind of a greeting's this?' Bobby Lee said.

'No greeting. That comes after you've stepped down and hung up your gunbelts.'

'Coffee and a plate of that stew would make the welcome a warm one,' Bobby Lee said.

He swung down, awkwardly unbuckled his belt and hung it on the saddle horn. As he stepped forward he could hear Blunt doing likewise, saw the tall man in front of him eyeing his bandages, the steady gaze searching his face. He chuckled softly.

'The wanted dodgers got the likeness all wrong, I'll wager you've never seen me in the flesh and I know damn well you couldn't see my face as I rode in. So tell me, how'd you know my name?'

'I was told to expect the Caprock Kid. Wounded.' The big man gestured towards the sky, and at Bobby Lee's shoulder. 'Clear moonlight, white sling supporting a damaged arm.'

'Told by who?'

'A certain Marshal Earp – no relation, he tells me, to the other one up in Ellsworth.'

'Someone,' Bobby Lee said, 'has been pullin' your tail.'

'Maybe,' the big man said. 'My name's Harlan Gibb. The lean man's Hobbs, Smoky's the feller trying to fatten him up with good grub. Why don't you move into the lamplight and tell us your side of the story.'

The cook wore a wool shirt, a derby hat and a long white apron covering most of his clothes. He was sitting on a box on the far side of the Dutch oven, leaning back against the chuck wagon. The shotgun he had cocked rested across his thighs. The long-limbed man called Hobbs was sitting cross-legged near the fire, smoking a cigarette. Maybe by accident or intent, his gunbelt had twisted around so that his hand rested carelessly against the butt of his six-gun. Bobby Lee had him pegged as the trail boss, figuring Gibb trusted him to make most of the decisions on the long drive.

Gibb sat down on a small keg and fired up a cigar. He pointed to the oven.

'Help yourself. Plates on the table.'

Up against the wagon, the cook spat his disgust into the fire.

Bobby Lee and Will Blunt collected plates and eating irons from the table, heaped the plates with grub from the pan in the Dutch oven and hunkered down near the fire. While they were eating like starved wolves the lean trail boss unwound his long frame and got up to pour two tin cups of coffee. He placed them on the grass close to Bobby Lee and Will, then wandered away from the fire to look down towards the herd and the moonlight gleaming on the Pecos.

The move wasn't lost on Bobby Lee. He and Will were now between the cook with his cocked shotgun and the trail boss and his worn-looking .44. Harlan Gibb was also taking everything in with an amused glint in his eyes.

He had a pistol, too, Bobby Lee noticed. If trouble started, they'd be caught in a three-way crossfire – and their own weapons were hanging from saddles thirty yards away.

'So don't start anything,' Harlan Gibb said, and Bobby Lee realized the rancher had been following his thoughts with uncanny accuracy.

'I don't know what else Marshal Earp told you,' Bobby Lee said, as he put the empty plate down by the full cup, 'but one of the men we're hunting robbed a bank in Amarillo, killed the marshal.' He looked steadily at Gibb. 'Seems to me that'd be one way of getting hold of a badge they could sort of pass around between 'em.'

'Why are you hunting them?'

'A man called Van Gelderen murdered my son. Another by the name of Cleet plugged me.' He touched his shoulder. 'A third murdered the son of a friend of mine, Chip Morgan. The son's name was Ed.'

'Ed Morgan's here, so you must be mistaken,' Gibb said. 'Ed will be guiding us across the plains.'

Bobby Lee ignored him.

'Ed Morgan was buried earlier today. Or maybe we're already talking about yesterday.' He shrugged. 'He was shot out of the saddle by a man who favours a long rifle. A buffalo gun.'

Out on the edge of the lamplight the trail boss snorted and turned to face the group.

'Smoky, you said you'd know him if you saw him.'

The cook grinned under his raking moustache.

'Yeah, and I'm loooking at him right now. B.L. Janson, the Caprock Kid. I seen him kill a man in a San Angelo gunfight. A stray bullet took a young girl's life – only the Kid was already hightailin' when she bit the dust—'

'What we've got,' Hobbs cut in, 'is one story from a man wearing a badge, an officer of the law, another from an outlaw who operates on the wrong side of that law and survives by lies and deception.'

'What you've got,' Will Blunt said, 'is some deci-sion-makin' to do – but before you get started, would someone please tell the feller in the over-sized apron to uncock his scattergun and point it the other way.'

Harlan Gibb smiled. 'Smoky.'

The hammers were lowered with an oily snick. The cook again spat into the fire. Then the shot-gun was lifted and propped against the wagon.

'I was on the subject of conflicting tales,' Harlan Gibb said. 'The first, coming from a man with a badge pinned to his vest, tells me to watch out for a man called B.L Janson. Janson bears me a grudge, the lawman says. He tells me I'd be well advised to watch out for my herd, and offers to provide an escort.'

'We've no reason to doubt him,' the lean trail boss said.

'The second comes from the aforementioned B.L. Janson, an outlaw,' Gibb continued. '*He* tells me the lawman is not what he seems. Apparently he's a man called Cleet, who robbed a bank in Amarillo, killed a town marshal and over the past couple of days has been involved in two more murders.'

'One of them was my son,' Bobbie Lee said. 'The other was the man you hired to guide you across the Staked Plains. The man in buckskins who rode into your camp was hired by Van Gelderen. He's an impostor.'

Gibb pulled a face. 'There's no way I can check that. Ed Morgan's name came to me word of mouth, I hired him through a third party so, until yesterday, I've never set eyes on him.

'One way out of the dilemma,' Harlan Gibb said, 'is to bring the two sides together. Hobbs, you know where Earp bedded down?'

'Nope. Last I saw, they were ridin' out.'

'How many is they?' Bobbie Lee said.

'Two. The marshal, and his companion with the long rifle.'

'The man with the long rifle murdered Ed Morgan. What about the marshal? Describe him for me.'

'Thickset. Unshaven. Pale eyes.'

'His real name's Cleet,' Bobby Lee said. 'He's the one put a hole in my shoulder.' He looked at Gibb. 'If they rode out, they're reporting back to Van Gelderen.'

He waited. It was the third time he'd dropped the outlaw's name into the conversation. On neither occasion had Gibb shown any reaction. Either his memory was short, or during the feud – if there had been one – Van Gelderen had been living under a different name.

'Impasse,' Gibb said. 'A classic stand-off. The only thing we know for sure – about you or the marshal, or whatever or whoever he is – is that Earp rode out. So now we set and wait. We settle this with you and him face to face.'

'Do that,' Bobbie Lee said, 'and you'll have cattle scattered halfway across three states.'

'You telling me there'll be gunplay?'

'Hah!' Bobbie Lee's laugh was a short bark. 'I've attended two funerals in as many days. Both victims were gunned down in cold blood, and you expect me to talk to the killers.'

'That's what you'll do,' Hobbs said, walking back into the firelight. 'From where I stand, you've got no choice.'

'From where I sit,' Will Blunt said, 'I'd argue the point. Stand-off's right, always has been. With that herd restin' easy out there but liable to jump at the slightest sound, gunplay's always been out of the question. Cookie's shotgun's useless; he knows it, you all know it – and that gives my puny little

85

weapon the power of a goddamn cannon.'

And for the second time that night a weapon was cocked. This time it was by Blunt. As he was talking he had casually pulled a Remington over-and-under .41 from his right boot. Now, with a broad grin on his face and his finger on the trigger, he was pointing it towards the star-lit skies.

ELEVEN

Bobbie Lee and her pa had been gone fifteen minutes. In that time the night fluttered with sound, but those sounds brought to Cassie the comfort of familiarity. Branches rattled overhead in the soft breeze. Leaves whispered. From time to time the undergrowth rustled at the passing of a small animal, and the distant keening of a coyote floated like a lament on the night air.

Cassie was unconcerned by the solitude, her only problem being how to pass the time until the two men returned. Knowing that Van Gelderen or one of his men might be out there, she used her blanket as camouflage. When she lay down on the dry grass and pulled the drab covering up over her head she knew that, tucked away in the hollow in deep shadows cast by the thin moonlight, she was just another bald, dun hummock.

Underneath the blanket, she felt safe and cosy. If anything, she was too hot. From time to time she poked her nose out to sniff the cool air. After the second or third time, blanket once again pulled over her, the heat and the quiet lulled her into a doze.

The different sound, when it came, was not startling. At first she thought it was Bobbie Lee and her pa riding back up the trail. Then, when she slipped the blanket down off her face and listened she realized that, although the sounds were undoubtedly made by a horse, this was no rider moving his mount with purpose.

He was moving slowly; pausing for some reason; then again coaxing his mount into a slow walk.

Puzzled, but still not alarmed, Cassie slipped completely out from under the blanket. She reached for the cold metal of the Henry, then wormed her way across the hollow. She reached the stony bank facing the trail. Eased her way close to the top. Stealthily cocked the Henry as she held her breath, poked the barrel over the bank then lifted her head, looked, and listened.

The very trees that had afforded concealment now blocked her view. She knew the trail was lit by moonlight – but she could see nothing. Her ears were her eyes. All her hearing was concentrated on the horse. She followed the unseen animal's erratic progress, her head turning slowly as she tracked movements she could not see.

The horse was moving to her right. Cassie flicked her eyes ahead. She saw a gap in the trees, through it a pool of wan moonlight lighting the trail. Her pulse quickened. The trail was no more than fifty feet from her. If the horse walked across that gap. . . .

Concentrating on that opening, on the patch of bright moonlight, she followed the horse's steps with her ears, listened as it drew closer, closer. . . .

Then – there it was! A head appeared, drooping to the trailing reins. Then the horse.

Riderless!

Cassie gasped. The horse was moving, unaccountably ignoring hanging reins that were meant to keep it ground-hitched. But why? Why was the horse continuing to walk, despite those trailing reins? Why would a man ground-hitch a horse when there were trees in abundance to which it could be tied?

And – where was the man?

Her skin prickled – and then she froze.

A cold ring of steel touched the back of her neck.

Cassie cried out.

An arm snaked round her neck. A rough hand clamped over her mouth and nose.

Overwhelmed by panic, careless of the pistol at her neck, Cassie began to fight. She whipped her head from side to side. Opened her mouth wide, moaning. Her teeth snapped shut – too late: the hand she was trying to bite was snatched away. She swung an elbow backwards. Her arm jarred against hard muscle. Then a leg was thrown across her. Weight bore down, pinning her to the bank. Whimpering, Cassie kicked her legs wildly. She writhed in the V of the man's straddling legs. Twisting, sliding, she squirmed around so that her back was hard against the bank.

The man straddling her was Van Gelderen. He was sitting back on his heels, his teeth bared in a savage grin. The muzzle of his six-gun was a black hole that seemed to be drawing her hypnotically into its gaping maw. Then, carelessly, knowing there was nothing she could do to save herself, he tilted it back so that it pointed up into the trees and eased down the hammer. His other hand reached out to pluck the Henry from her grasp and, with a quick flip, he tossed it end-over-end into the bushes.

TWELVE

It was Will Blunt who found the rifle. From the moment they got back to the hollow he was a wild animal on the prowl, first picking up the crumpled blankets as if expecting to find Cassie beneath them and looking stunned when she wasn't, then studying the soft ground inside the hollow and the faint imprint of horses' hooves on the hard, dusty trail before crackling his way back through the woods with his eyes sweeping to left and right.

When he stopped suddenly and bent to pick up the Henry it was with a muttered exclamation that could have been triumph or despair. Eyes flashing fiercely, he brandished it aloft so that the barrel glittered in the moonlight, then cut across to where Bobbie Lee was waiting in the hollow with the horses.

'Tells us nothing we didn't already know,' Bobby Lee said. 'Van Gelderen used trickery and caught her cold.'

'The only way she *could* be caught,' Will said. 'From the signs I'd say the bastard crept up behind

91

her when she was distracted by something or someone.'

'But why? Why take her?'

'A hostage. They think by holding her under
threat of death we'll stay well clear while they deal
with Gibb and his herd.'

'And they're wrong?'

'Damn right they are. Oh, the threat's real, but
we're going after her.'

'No, we're not.'

'Oh, for Christ's sake, Bobbie Lee—'

'All right, go after her where?'

'I don't know. We ride, we search—'

'Where? Where do you start?'

'Where do I start? I thought we were in this
together?'

'We are. But chasing shadows gets us nowhere.
Hell, they're not even shadows; Van Gelderen
could be just about anywhere—'

'Then we search anywhere and *everywhere* until
we find her. And if you're out of it, then I'll go
alone.'

'I've got a better idea.'

Blunt had already turned away and started for
his horse. But Bobby Lee knew his friend had the
kind of anger that could disperse as fast as thin
mist in a high wind, and an inqusitive nature that
would never let him walk away from an intriguing
statement.

He stopped, half turned, his eyes guarded.

'It'd better be good.'

'It is. What we do is, we play along.'

Now it was Blunt's turn to ask the questions, and the humour of the situation didn't escape him. A thin smile flickered across his lean countenance.

'All right. Play along how?'

'If they're holding Cassie to keep us away, then that's what we do.'

'I'm ahead of you. I know how your mind works. Your idea is to track the herd, but stay out of sight.' He shook his head. 'Won't work.'

'Why?'

'Cleet and the feller with the buff' gun will stay with the herd, so foolin' them should be no problem. But what about Van Gelderen? He's the one holding Cassie, and you said yourself we have no idea where he is. He could be a mile away, a hundred yards away, and we've no way of knowing.'

Bobbie Lee nodded thoughtfully. High clouds had drifted across the moon. In the hollow it was as if the flame of an oil lamp had been blown out. He sat down on a log and pulled out the makings, rolled a cigarette then tossed the sack and papers to Blunt. While the other man rolled his smoke and paced restlessly across the hollow, Bobbie Lee took a closer look at the situation.

Blunt was right. The herd would string out across the Staked Plains, with the man in buckskins leading the way and Cleet and his murderous *compadre* tagging along. Van Gelderen had to stay out of sight for fear of being recognized. But – and this was where Bobbie Lee could see a glimmer of hope – if Van Gelderen was going to be in at the kill, the stampede, then he had to stay close.

But then, as a match flared and the flat plains and angles of Blunt's face were thrown into harsh relief, Bobbie Lee found himself questioning their own flimsy planning. Their objective was to apprehend the killers of Jason and Ed Morgan, yet they'd left the Halt without any idea of how they were to going to achieve that aim.

'We've been riding blind, so to speak,' he said softly, and caught the movement in the gloom as Blunt lifted his head and looked across at him.

'Meaning?'

'We're after the killers. We rode out of the Halt with clear intentions, but no plan. We found the herd, explained the situation to Harlan Gibb and he's neither for us nor against us because he can't be sure who's telling the truth. But who the hell cares what he thinks? When that herd starts across the Staked Plains, Gibb and his crew will have their own worries looking after two thousand thirsty animals heading north under a blazing sun. Seems to me we can do what the hell we like, when we like—'

'Not any more we can't.'

Bobbie Lee's mild tirade was cut short. He looked down at the glowing tip of his cigarette, his eyes narrowed – and he knew that, once again, Will Blunt had got it right. It didn't matter what their plans had or hadn't been: Van Gelderen had changed everything by snatching Cassie.

They were back where they were when they rode into the hollow and found it empty of life, and at least then Bobbie Lee had been thinking straight: they didn't know where Van Gelderen was holding the woman, and they had no idea how to commence looking for her. Until they got that solved, their hands were tied.

'So what now, Will?'

Blunt's cigarette glowed as he took a long pull.

'Maybe Cassie can do something.'

'You serious?'

'Remember what I did back there?'

'Sure. Pulled a pistol from your—'

Bobbie Lee stopped and took a deep breath. When he let it out, it had turned into a chuckle of delighted disbelief.

'Please, tell me you're joshing, Will.'

'Nope. They came as a pair, those beauties. The second of 'em is down in my little girl's right boot – and she's always been a sight faster than I am at pulling that little .41 out into the daylight and firing off both barrels.'

They spent the night in the hollow, Will Blunt wrapped in his own blankets but with Cassie's close enough for him to touch. From his position tucked in against a hummock on the other side of the dying embers of the fire on which they'd cooked their supper, Bobbie Lee watched him several times hold those blankets to his nose, his big fist white-knuckled. He didn't know whether his friend could detect in the crumpled folds his daughter's scent, but he knew for sure that merely holding them close was a comfort to the other man.

The next morning breakfast was another simple meal eaten by the fire, consisting mostly of jerky washed down by several tin cups of scalding coffee drunk in a hollow shrouded in mist and with the blankets they had slept in draped around their shoulders. It was taken early. Five- or six-o'clock. And after it they sat smoking, drawn close up to the crackling flames, and tried to work out their next move.

'Stay back from the herd,' Bobbie Lee said, after a long, contemplative silence. 'That's what Van Gelderen wants; he's got Cassie, so that's what we'll do.'

'Way back,' Will Blunt said, eyes narrowed and distant in thought. 'Back so far we can see the herd move. Back so far we can watch the last of the drag riders tidying up the tail.' He turned to look at Bobby Lee. 'Back so far we can watch that bastard Van Gelderen tag on behind – because that's what he'll do – and I can maybe get a long, clear shot at him with the Sharps.'

'Is that wise?'

'A long rifle knocked Ed Morgan out of the saddle; another can do the same to Van Gelderen.'

'Different circumstance,' Bobbie Lee said, and let Blunt chew on it.

In a tense silence they both pondered on that thought, each man knowing that the risks were enormous, each looking for a way round those risks. Van Gelderen had Cassie, and he would be smart enough to keep her close to him. To avoid being seen, Bobby Lee knew he and Will would be

forced to ride something like half a mile behind
the outlaw; maybe more than that. At that
distance, on the Staked Plains, the heat rising from
yard upon yard of hard-packed desert would create
a wicked, shimmering heat haze. A target viewed
through that would be there then gone, jumping
about like a flea on a string, most of the time more
mirage than reality. Add to those difficulties the
possibility of a searing cross wind, and at that
distance – anything from eight hundred to one
thousand yards – it would take a brave man or a
fool to try to drop one of a pair of riders.

'We wait,' Will Blunt said flatly.

'Our time will come.'

Will grinned ruefully. 'Yeah, and I reckon that
pronouncement can be taken in a number of ways,
not all of them guaranteed to lift a man's spirits.'

The way Bobbie Lee had it figured, Harlan Gibb
would get his men fed in the late afternoon,
ensure his rested livestock had taken their fill of
water from the deep, slow-moving Pecos then
point them towards the desert as the sun went
down. He would push them hard, putting as many
miles behind them as he could before sun-up the
next day. Trouble was, a man could wear his
'punchers to a frazzle trying to get speed out of a
bunch of cattle, and at the end of a long night still
wind up just twelve or so miles from the starting
point.

That left an awful lot of desert to be covered.
And, on the Llano Estacado, letting the herd rest

during the heat of the day was liable to prove fatal. There was no shade. All that happened was the cattle got dehydrated and went crazy while stationary instead of on the move. Dying was less of an effort, but just as permanent.

Those thoughts, and many others, were there to intrigue Will and Bobbie Lee as they washed the breakfast plates and looked ahead at a long day of inactivity.

According to Will Blunt, it was the lull before the storm.

Before they left the Halt they'd been astute enough to share the extra water bottles among the three of them. Cassie's would be almost untouched. Bobbie Lee and Will had used more than a couple of pints for supper and breakfast, and so had at least one empty. Knowing it would be foolish to start across the desert short of water, Bobbie Lee rode out later that morning to refill their bottles. He deliberately rode south and west, heading towards the Pecos River some way downstream of the herd so that he could observe the situation.

He tethered his horse in a stand of cottonwoods, filled the bottles from a bend in the river were the water was clear, and once they were safe in the saddle-bags he looked around for some high ground. The land was gently undulating, and that was in his favour; when he walked up a low rise and gazed north, he had a clear view of the distant herd.

As he'd expected, there was little sign of life.

With the aid of a battered pair of army field-glasses he could pick out a couple of 'punchers who were doing nothing more than ride the herd's perimeter keeping a watchful eye out for strays. But Gibb's trail boss had picked his last stop with care. If any animals did take it into their heads to roam, they would most likely sniff the air and trot down to the Pecos – which was exactly what Gibb wanted.

By shifting the glasses, Bobbie Lee could see the chuck-wagon. A thin column of smoke was rising from the fire, but here too there was a whole lot of nothing happening. Up in the trees near the wagon – too shaded for Bobby Lee to make out with any certainty – there were shapes he knew must be the rest of Gibb's cowpokes, either still sleeping, looking to their equipment, or lazily playing cards. He *could* see a figure over by the remuda, and guessed the wrangler was one of the few men raising a sweat.

Of Cleet and the man with the buffalo gun there was no sign at all – but, hell, Bobbie Lee thought as he turned away in disgust, I'm a goddamn mile away and here I am trying to pick out individuals.

It took him a half-hour to ride back to the hollow. He could smell the smoke and coffee a quarter-mile away. When he'd pulled in and unsaddled his horse he told Will Blunt what he had seen from the rise. Will agreed that Bobbie Lee had probably found the ideal spot from which to start their night ride. A long way back from the herd, with plenty of space for Van Gelderen and his hostage to slot in between.

99

With that major decision taken care of, they finished off the coffee and prepared to bed down under the trees for the afternoon. They intended to ride out, and be in position long before dusk. And Bobbie Lee's last recollection before he drifted off to sleep with clouds of flies droning hypnotically in the intense heat was the sight of Will Blunt with the Sharps rifle across his knees and his tongue sticking out as he applied oil to the weapon's breech with a soft rag.

THIRTEEN

Cassie was some yards into a thin stand of parched trees, sitting in the shade with her back against a twisted trunk, her ankles hobbled.

Me and my horse, she thought ruefully, glancing across at the tethered pony. Two of a kind, stuck here while those three sit chewing the fat around the camp-fire – and again she marvelled at the ingenuity of Van Gelderen, who had left her hands free, used thin rawhide bindings to restrict her leg movement and poured water over the knot so that it tightened and would be impossible to unpick.

After the terrifying assault when she had stared into the muzzle of Van Gelderen's six-gun, they had ridden north and west from the hollow and camped when the sun was a band of dazzling light stretching across the horizon – Cassie linked to Van Gelderen by a length of rope that connected their ankles and made her escape impossible.

She had estimated that on that night ride the outlaw had been pushing towards the Llano Estacado's eastern escarpment. The realization set her wondering what Bobbie Lee and her pa had planned. Clearly, those plans would, to a great extent, depend on the location of the outlaws. Cassie was with the leader of the bunch and, from where he'd made camp, she assumed he intended riding up onto the Staked Plains through one of the jagged gullies splitting those eastern heights. That would bring him onto the plain some way to the east of the cattle drive.

Trouble was, she had no way of getting that information to Bobby Lee, nor any way of knowing what Bobby Lee and her pa had found out when they left her to ride to the herd in search of the truth. If there was a herd. And, assuming there was, if the rancher they were hoping to meet knew what the hell they were talking about.

Her jumbled thoughts were abruptly interrupted. Van Gelderen had leaped to his feet. With a flick of the wrist he sent the dregs of his coffee hissing into the fire. The thud of hooves had announced the approach of a rider in a hurry. Feeling her pulse quicken, Cassie prepared to do some listening.

'This'll be Callaghan,' Van Gelderen said.

Moments later, the buckskin-clad outlaw who had left the Halt before the others came racing round a bend and rode hard into the camp. Close to the trees he pulled his horse to a sliding stop. He slid from the saddle and moved to the fire, slapping clouds of trail dust from his clothes. He nodded to Cleet and the man with the buffalo gun, and grinned happily at Van Gelderen.

'That's it done. She's all set.'

'No problems? Nobody there who knew the real Morgan by sight?'

'Nope. And Gibb moves his herd at sundown. Right now he thinks I'm out there on the plains blazing a trail – though Christ knows where he got the idea you need a brilliant plan to cross a featureless desert.'

'Maybe he's hoping you can use those mysterious Comanche water-holes as steppin' stones,' Cleet said.

'Yeah, I've heard there's a couple out there,' Callaghan said. 'Me, I'm from the south, and knowledge of any water-holes up this way conveniently died when Sangster shot the Morgan boy.'

He walked to the fire, found himself a tin cup in the ashes up against the ring of stones and poured coffee from the pot.

'You want bringing up to date?'

'I'd guess not much happened,' Van Gelderen said. 'I can't see Gibb swallowing Janson's story after the show ol' Cleet tells me he put on.'

Callagan was hunkered down, grinning over his coffee.

'I was close enough to hear most of it. And I heard everything Gibb said afterwards when Janson rode in. The rancher was willing to listen, but wanted Marshal Earp there with Janson so he could get both sides of the story with them face to face – only Earp and his pard had turned into a couple of ghosts.'

'Ghost riders,' Cleet said, 'out on the trail. Once this pow-wow's over we'll ride back with you. Old pals. You to show Gibb the trail to nowhere; me and Sangster there to stop the wicked Caprock Kid from frightening his cows.'

Van Gelderen chuckled.

'You and Callaghan'll ride in first, Sangster will follow later. Before that I've got another job suited to our friend's unique talents with that rifle.' He nodded in the direction of the woods. 'Janson and that woman's pa are out there—'

'Damn right they are,' Callaghan cut in. 'Gibb made sure they hung up their guns, but Blunt pulled a hideaway pistol from his boot and threatened them with a stampede.'

'Gibb should have paid attention, because that's exactly what's going to happen,' Van Gelderen said. He looked across at Sangster. 'It's just a pity Blunt and the Kid won't be there to see it.'

The rifleman smiled.

'You want me to find them, I'll do that. You want me to make sure there's two riderless horses – I'll do that too.'

'Cold-blooded bastard.' Van Gelderen's grin was cruel, his eyes thoughtful.

'There'll be a full moon tonight,' Sangster said. 'Like cold daylight. but even if that don't work out right, even if there's cloud over the moon. . . .' He shrugged. 'I'm as good with a pistol as with that big buff' gun. All it means is I get closer, maybe they'll see me in the last seconds of their miserable lives.'

Van Gelderen's fingers tapped the empty cup.

'It's easy enough to work out where they'll be. Janson knows Gibb is not happy with him, and he knows I've got Blunt's girl. That threat could cause him and Blunt to think twice about coming after me. But I don't really believe it. The way I see it, all it'll do is make them more cautious. But that works in our favour. When the herd moves out, they'll hang back. They'll be watching for me, wondering what the hell I'm going to do. They won't be expecting danger because they believe you, Cleet and Murphy will be with the herd.'

'Two-thirds right,' Sangster said.

'The one third they're wrong will prove fatal.' Van Gelderen eyes were gleaming with a strange light. 'The Caprock Kid'll be out of my life, out of my waking nightmares. Dead and buried. The debt finally paid, snuffed out by his last, dying breath.'

'Because I'll be out there,' Sangster said, 'watching the watchers.'

'But not for too long.'

'Just long enough to get them in my sights,' Sangster said. 'Squeeze off a couple of shots. Then, yeah, all your troubles'll be over.'

In the woods, despite the heat of the afternoon, Cassie Blunt was frozen with horror. She had listened and learned names, got a hazy idea of what had gone on when Bobby Lee and her pa had talked to the rancher, and from where she sat could see the badge shining on Cleet's vest.

The outlaws had used that badge to gain credibility in the rancher's eyes. The story they had told had blackened Bobbie Lee's name. Cassie guessed they had simply told the rancher – Gibb – exactly what was planned, but named Bobbie Lee as the troublemaker, the man bearing a grudge. If he believed that, Gibb would always be looking the wrong way; always searching the scorching plains for trouble when trouble was riding with him.

But the rancher's problems were as nothing compared with those facing Bobbie Lee and her pa.

Staring out through the trees at the outlaws, Cassie's eyes blurred with tears. She'd just heard two men pass sentence of death on the men she loved and there was nothing she could do about it.

Or was there?

Biting her lip, she watched the men gathered around the fire. The one called Cleet had gone across to his saddle-bags and returned with a bottle of whiskey. The bottle was being passed around. Nobody was paying her any attention.

She looked across at her pony. No more than thirty yards away from her, it was loosely tethered to a tree. A pull on their loose ends would free the reins. No tight rawhide there to be unpicked.

Her Hobbsles were a different matter. They could not be untied. She had no knife. With the hobbles in place she could not ride the pony even if she could reach it.

But that, Cassie decided, was the thinking of a defeatist.

If she did reach the pony, it could be ridden. She'd heard of ladies' side-saddles. If a lady could use a special saddle to ride with both her legs on the same side of the horse, then by heck she, Cassie Blunt, could do the same without any goddamn special saddle.

And if the outlaws looked around, caught her in no-man's-land somewhere between the tree and her pony – then they were in for one hell of a surprise. Because didn't she still have that little over-and-under Remington .41 tucked down all snug in her boot?

Damn right she did.

She chuckled softly, quickly smothering the laugh with her hand.

Van Gelderen had taken her arms in his iron grip, forced her down against the tree, dropped to his knees in front of her and used the length of skinny rawhide to make a hobble. His hands had been all over her ankles as he worked – and still he'd missed the bulge of the pistol.

For that slip, he would pay dear.

Cassie took a deep breath. She cast a final glance towards the camp-fire as harsh guffaws rang out, saw the bottle tossed glittering across the now dancing flames. Then she made her move.

No time for pussyfooting. She moved fast, decisively. From the awkward seated position she rolled, came to her knees then sprang to her feet. With both hands on the coarse bark, she swung herself behind the tree. She was breathing hard but controlling it. Her mouth was open so there was no hiss of breath.

It was a solid fact, she knew, that movement

drew the eye while stillness went unnoticed. The prisoner was no longer sitting cross-legged, but her first swift movements had been missed. Now the advantage lay with her. There were several trees between her and the pony. As she crossed those thirty yards – which looked uncomfortably like thirty miles – she would ensure they were between her and the outlaws.

But how should she move?

Biting her lip, Cassie tried a pace, then another. Short paces. Paces restricted as the rawhide snapped taut. The alternative was a series of awkward double-legged hops, but that could be noisy, and she'd be risking a fall.

Reckless speed, and to hell with it? – or a duck-like waddle that would set her nerves screaming with impatience and fear?

Cassie waddled.

It was like exposing herself in the slots of those new-fangled moving picture machines she'd heard about, and she had to clench her teeth to hold back a giggle. She'd pass a tree, through the gap get a glimpse of the outlaws around the camp-fire, then the next tree would block her view. She went through that half-a-dozen times; seven trees, six gaps through which her progress might be glimpsed – and then she steppd one last time, stumbled, and fell against the startled pony; clapped a hand over its warm muzzle; whispered soothing words of comfort.

She'd reached her mount, but every second that passed brought discovery closer. And even as she cupped the pony's muzzle and whispered those soothing words she knew she had blundered. Yes, she could walk after a fashion, hop all through the long hot day, even ride sideways-on without a special saddle – but first she had to climb up on the horse. Compared with the struggle that lay ahead, making it to the pony had been a cakewalk – and she was running out of time.

Breathing deeply, salty sweat trickling into her eyes, Cassie kept her hand on the excited pony as she looked back towards the camp-fire. All she could see was the smoke rising above the trees. The outlaws were hidden by the trees and so couldn't see her – thank God!

But they could see the tree where she'd been sitting, and if they looked that way now . . .

Desperation threatened to turn to panic. Her hand was clutching the saddle horn. She was breathing in shallow gasps. Suddenly her legs felt weak. Frantically she tried to think, but as her eyes darted wildly as if seeking inspiration she could see no way of hoisting herself up onto the horse without floundering and finishing up belly down and creating enough commotion to stampede that goddamn herd never mind warn the outlaws.

And then she saw her saddle-bags. Almost under her nose. In them she had stowed water bottles, some food and clothing – and her clasp knife!

Move!

Relief flooded through her, bringing with it strength. She snatched her hand from the pony's

muzzle. Fumbling, her fingers like those of someone already dead, she unbuckled the flap and
thrust her hand inside the soft leather. The knife
was there. She bit her bottom lip, hope soaring,
brought the knife out and snapped open the
blade. Then she bent down and sliced, sliced,
sliced through the hobble's tough leather.

Sensing her excitement, the pony turned its
head and whickered.

'Oh, no!' Cassie whispered.

She slipped the knife into her pocket, jerked the
end of the reins to undo the hitch and swung
lithely into the saddle. Rawhide trailed from each
ankle as she thrust her feet into the stirrups.
Saying a silent prayer that the outlaws had taken
that whicker to come from one of their own
horses, she nudged the pony's flanks with her
heels and urged it into the trees. If she could get
through them, out the other side into open
ground . . .

The trees closed in. As the pony leaped forward,
a branch snapped. The sound was like a gunshot.
Cassie's mouth opened wide in a silent gasp of
horror.

Behind her someone yelled, 'Christ, the
woman's gettin' away!' and seconds later the
undergrowth crackled under pounding feet and
there was another loud bang. This time it was a
gunshot. The bullet, aimed at the horse, rico-
cheted off a stone and howled into the sky.

Then Cassie was lying flat along the racing
pony's neck, the hairs of its streaming mane flying

in her narrowed eyes as she spurred recklessly for the relative safety of the open ground that lay beyond the edge of the trees.

FOURTEEN

An hour after sundown. To the west, the last of the light was still flaring red in the skies above the Guadaloupe Mountains, but perceptibly fading. As dusk crept over the plains like the shadow of a storm advancing from the east, Bobbie Lee and Will Blunt saddled the sorrel and the skinny blue roan and broke camp. It was a clear night with just a faint breeze, but Bobbie Lee had a feeling in his bones that boded ill. Those disturbing thoughts were in his mind as they cantered out of the hollow and pointed their horses south. As they did so, Blunt gestured urgently with his hand. Bobbie Lee looked across the open plain and saw the perfect orb of the rising moon.

'Helps us,' he said. 'Gibb and his men will be gazing north. Any not doing that'll be too busy chasing strays to see us, but with that moon there'll be nowhere for Van Gelderen to hide.'

'That may be, but somehow I can't see a feller that mean allowing us to roam free,' Will Blunt said, and then Bobbie Lee knew that his vague uneasiness was justified.

As they rode they could hear distant yips and hollers, and the angry bellowing of cattle as Gibb and his crew worked to get two thousand reluctant animals up on their feet and moving. With those sounds in their ears they rode steadily, ruminating on what might lie ahead but moving swiftly across country until they reached the spot Bobbie Lee had earmarked. In that undulating region the shadows were long. On their western flank the Pecos River glittered under a veil of thin mist.

They pulled in under the cottonwoods. Bobbie Lee dug out his field-glasses, squinted through them, got the focus right and peered north. Despite the fading light he could see the dust cloud already billowing, the dark shapes that were riders on the flanks of the extended, rolling mass of the slowly moving herd. Shifting the glasses, he looked for any sign of movement that would reveal the presence of two riders in the area behind the herd. He looked until his eyes watered with the strain, but saw nothing

'I think we figured this all wrong,' Blunt said.

For a few moments Bobbie Lee said nothing. He was thinking back over the decisions they'd made. The way they'd worked everything out. They'd been right about the herd. They knew for certain the man in buckskins had taken Ed Morgan's name and his job, and Cleet was using a stolen tin badge to work it so he could justify being close to Harlan Gibb at all times. Maybe they should have gone along with the big rancher, faced Cleet and let Gibb decide who was telling the truth. But that would never have worked. Cleet had more people to back up his story. Bobby Lee had already admitted he was the Caprock Kid, and been recognized as such by the cook – and in any case, Cleet and his companion could not be found. So Will had pulled a gun and they'd made their escape and if that hadn't settled Gibb's mind, then nothing would.

Maybe, Bobby Lee thought, that was when everything started to go wrong. Their thinking had gone south, and they'd been so certain Van Gelderen would do the same they'd ridden in that direction to put themselves behind the herd.

He sighed.

'If you were Van Gelderen, holding a valuable hostage, knowing damn well her pa and another man are out there looking for you – what would you do?'

'Stay out of sight,' Blunt said. 'Or if I had a fair idea of the whereabouts of the people hunting me, ride like hell in the opposite direction, put distance between us.'

'And what would you do,' Bobby Lee said, 'if there was a big horse fly buzzing around your ears annoying the hell out of you?'

'Swat it.'

'Or, if you were going someplace else, get someone to do it for you.'

'Someone,' Will Blunt said, 'unlikely to miss.'

'I don't know about you,' Bobby Lee said, 'but I've got a sudden itchy feeling in the middle of my back.'

*

What they hadn't accounted for, the gunman realized, was the effect of the booming shots when he pulled the big rifle's trigger.

He'd ridden slow and steady from Van Gelderen's campsite until he was below the herd, picked a spot on the western bank of the Pecos and swum his horse across. The way he had it figured, Janson and Blunt would stay on the opposite bank.

He was right. His clothes were almost dry when he'd spotted them approaching the river. Now they'd eased their horses back into the cottonwoods. Sangster caught a brief flash of light, the wink of the setting sun on glass, and reckoned one of them was using field-glasses. They were watching the herd – or watching for something. But if they looked across the river to his position they'd be gazing into the setting sun – glasses or no glasses – while he'd have the sun at his back and a couple of easy shots at clearly visible targets.

Problem was, two shots from the powerful buff' gun were likely to spook the herd – and that would ruin Van Gelderen's precious plans.

Hunkered down in a grove of alder, cigarette glowing in his cupped hand, Sangster debated his dilemma. Shoot the bastards with the big gun, and to hell with it? – or get close enough to . . . to what?

A six-gun at close range was just as likely to cause a stampede, especially if he needed more than a couple of shots to do the job. He had a knife in his boot, but could he get close enough for a silent kill? Hell, he was no damn Injun and, even if he got there, one of the men he was going up against was the Caprock Kid.

Call the whole thing off?

Maybe. Van Gelderen would be no worse off, the herd would be moving, and in a couple of days it'd be just where he wanted it.

The snag was that would leave Janson and Blunt on the loose, and it was never a good idea to cross Van Gelderen. If the man sent you out to blow a couple of fellers out of the saddle – that's what you did. One way or another. And, looked at coldly, logically, the only way that could be done without spooking the herd was to get close.

Maybe, Sangster thought, the six-gun was the best option. He lifted his head and looked north. The breeze was blowing in his face, the herd more than a mile upwind with noise all around them. Maybe the crack of a six-gun would go unheard. Or maybe – and here a sour grin crossed Sangster's face – maybe he should think about getting himself one of those Remington bean-shooters Blunt had pulled on Harlan Gibb. A couple of pops and the job'd be done.

But he *didn't* have one – and now there were a whole lot of maybes tossed into the pot and suddenly Sangster's guts were crawling with nerves.

With a soft, muttered curse, he stubbed out his cigarette, climbed to his feet and went to untie his horse.

As he swung into the saddle he could see in the

fading light that Janson and Blunt were still waiting in the cottonwoods. Aware that they could at any moment look in his direction he swung west and, using the shelter of a small rise, made for the river in a wide, swinging circle. When his horse slithered down the bank and splashed into the water he was some fifty yards below the cottonwoods, the stand of trees between him and the two men.

He made the crossing without raising the alarm, out of the saddle and up to his neck in water, clinging to the slick horn, his boots and weapons held high out of the river. When he clambered up the opposite bank he was, for the second time that night, streaming muddy water. His socks squelched as he slid his feet into his boots.

He spat in disgust. Strapped on his gunbelt. Checked his .45. Jogged to the trees and tethered his horse out of sight.

Now what? Risk the snap of branches by stumbling blind through the woods, or play safe and circle around in the open?

He chose the longer, quieter way, creeping along the Pecos side of the cottonwoods so that the whisper of boots in the grass would blend with the soft lapping of the water. When he looked west the reflection of the night skies turned the river blood red beneath the veil of mist. Behind him the moon was beginning to throw its light across the plains, and already his shadow was moving ahead of him.

Sangster drew back his lips as he saw it, and instantly hugged the trees. He was close enough now to hear the murmur of two men talking; saw through the last of the trees – with an urgent and worried glance – the darker shapes that could only be two riders, two horses. His six-gun made a sibilant sound as it cleared supple leather. There was a muted, oily click as he eased back the hammer.

He froze, not breathing. Heard the creak of leather as one of the men turned in the saddle. A face gleamed pale in the moonlight. Not daring to wait Sangster clenched his teeth, lifted the six-gun high and stepped swiftly around the trees.

'That's all, gentlemen,' he said. 'Don't either one of you move a single damn muscle.'

FIFTEEN

The last of the sunlight had gone. Above the Guadaloupe Mountains the sky was a dull red. The gunman had stepped out of the shelter of the woods and cunningly put his back to that lurid glow, but the light from the moon was already sufficient for Bobbie Lee to see his face. And the glitter of the pistol.

He immediately recognized the weapon as a Colt .45 and, as he had done so many times before, Bobby Lee smiled inwardly at the amazing ability with which he had been blessed. It was the ability to take in the smallest of details in moments of great crisis, and while one part of his mind was observing, another separate part would be examining possibilities, looking for actions that would enable him to wriggle out of an impossible situation.

The sound he had heard only seconds ago had been the cocking of that Colt .45. The pistol was now being aimed at a point just above the bridge of his nose by the man called Sangster, the man skilful enough with a firearm to gun down Ed Morgan, in cold blood, at a range of more than half a mile.

This situation was dire.

If he had gunned down Ed Morgan in that manner, what qualms might he now have that would deter him from pulling the trigger and blowing first Bobbie Lee, then Will Blunt, into the next world?

None at all. And because there was no possible way that Bobbie Lee could draw his gun fast enough to beat a man with his finger already squeezing the trigger of a cocked pistol, the razor-sharp mind that was working on possibilities that did not exist began to look at reality – and found it to be an unsavoury and sobering task.

'You stand there much longer holding that big pistol,' Will Blunt was saying conversationally, 'your arm's going to get tired and what'll you do then?'

Bobbie Lee forced a chuckle. 'He'll swap hands. Faster than the eye can see. He's a real tough character, this one.'

'Long before that happens,' Sangster said, 'you'll both be dead.'

'Is that what this is about?'

'What d'you think? Target practice? You think I'm here to shoot your hat full of holes?'

Bobbie Lee grinned and looked across at Blunt.

'What I think is he likes shooting his mouth off – right, Will.'

'A man who talks too much is putting off the

main event,' Blunt said. 'This feller can shoot a man out of the saddle at a thousand yards, but when he's forced to look that man in the eye his backbone turns to water.'

'Tell me,' Sangster said, 'are these your last words I'm hearing?'

'No, you tell me,' Blunt said, and spat into the grass. 'Squeeze that trigger, Mr Bushwhacker, and prove to me that I'm wrong.'

Bobbie Lee felt himself stiffen. Talk had seemed to be the only way out. Will had come to the same conclusion and spoken first, but his last words seemed to have thrown away the advantage. He'd pushed Sangster too far; Christ, he'd *reminded* him what he was there for: he'd been sent by Van Gelderen to get Bobbie Lee and Blunt out of his hair – and Will had coolly told him to get on with it.

Almost imperceptibly, the pistol's barrel shifted. That was all it took, a slight adjustment to the aim. But now it was pointing at Will Blunt. Now Sangster's teeth were bared in a savage grin and, even from ten feet away, Bobbie Lee could see his knuckle whiten inside the trigger guard.

'Go ahead,' Will said blandly. 'Pull the trigger.'

The shot rang out.

Bobbie Lee's heart leaped. His horse threw up its head and pranced backwards, rocking him in the saddle.

As he clung to the taut reins, fought to keep his seat and watched in amazement, Sangster wobbled backwards. His arm lost all its strength and fell to

121

his side. The pistol dropped from his fingers. His eyes bulged with shock, and the dark stain of blood was spreading across his shirt front. He tried to walk even as he was falling, and then he was staggering down the bank and there was a splash and a gout of glittering water shot into the moonlight as his legs crumpled and he fell flat on his back in the river.

'You knew, Will,' Bobbie Lee said accusingly. 'But how the hell did you? And why not give me some sign, some warning, instead of baiting the man like that and almost giving me a seizure?'

They were down off their horses. Will Blunt was holding Cassie in his arms. Her face was buried in his shoulder. Her right arm was by her side, her hand still clutching the Remington over-and-under .41 that had done for Sangster.

'My powers of observation,' Will said slyly. 'You were fallin' asleep listenin' to him, but I saw her come walkin' around them trees on that pony. I saw that little pistol in her hand. I was just about scared rigid, but she put a finger to her lips telling me to keep quiet as if everything was under control.' He shrugged, grinning like a fool.

'With that two-shot pistol,' Bobbie Lee said, 'I'd be lucky to hit the side of a mountain from the inside of a box canyon. Your little girl plugged him plumb centre.'

'Some little girl,' Will said, and let Cassie pull away from his grasp.

'I heard those outlaws talking, Bobbie Lee,' she

said. 'I knew what Sangster was going to do tonight – and I think I sort of know why.'

'You sound unsure, but ain't that the easy bit?' Bobbie Lee said. 'Van Gelderen wants us out of the way so he can get on with destroying Harlan Gibb. That's it, isn't it?'

'A big part of it. But not all.'

'So tell us the rest.

She had walked across to Bobbie Lee and now reached up to touch his face. It was almost as if she'd not expected to see him, ever again, Bobbie Lee thought – and that realization and her obvious pleasure at being wrong gave him a warm glow that took him completely by surprise.

Not Cassie. She was gazing into his eyes, and a knowing smile parted her lips as his feelings became clear. She ran the backs of her fingers down his stubbly chin, lightly touched the tip of his nose, then stepped away and turned serious.

'As far as I can recall, Van Gelderen was talking to Sangster. He was saying you wouldn't expect trouble because you believed all three of them – Murphy, Cleet and Sangster – were staying with the herd. But Sangster said you were only two thirds right, because he was coming after you.' She frowned. 'And then Van Gelderen said, when you were dead the debt would be paid in full. His exact words, I think, were "snuffed out with your last dying breath".'

'I have never in my life seen that man before he rode into the Halt,' Bobbie Lee said.

'Then forget it,' Blunt said. 'His reasons for

doing things don't in any way excuse the things he's done. I reckon that sounds like I've been eating some of that loco weed, doesn't it? Well, I guess that's because I'm still trying to figure out how Cassie got away from that bastard.'

'Walked and rode,' Cassie said. 'They were jawing away, I cut the rawhide' – she waggled a foot in the air to show them the leather strip dangling from her boot – 'and left them chasing each other's tails.'

'Yeah,' Will Blunt said, 'you always could outride and outshoot the young males in the Halt.'

'You mean Zeke and Ed Morgan,' Cassie said softly. She was quiet for a moment. Then, as if recalling the young friend who had been cruelly gunned down had jogged her memory, she said, 'Pa, did you find my Henry?'

'Found the herd, met the rancher, used the second of those pistols to make a getaway, found your Henry in that godawful hollow – yeah, we've got it. We've also got a lot of catching up to do, and some serious planning.'

'Damn right,' Bobbie Lee said. 'Gibb is busy moving his herd onto the Llano Estacado. What we've got to do is decide what the hell we're going to do next.'

SIXTEEN

They talked around a small fire Bobbie Lee built in a circle of stones on the bank of the Pecos. Cassie shivered at disturbing thoughts and deliberately sat cross-legged with her back to the river; Sangster's body had floated off into the mists, but had been slow doing so and in a silence made eerie by his death his gruesome memory lingered.

Will Blunt brewed coffee, Cassie broke out some of the jerky she had in her saddle-bags, and after a while Bobbie Lee again went to the river bend and refilled the water bottles. When he returned, he joined the others by the fire with a cigarette glowing in his fist.

'First subject to discuss is the herd,' he said. 'Will, you mentioned the Goodnight-Loving trail back in the Halt, and that pointed us in the right direction. But as far as I can see, they're off course. Charlie Goodnight came up the west bank of the Pecos. He took his herd across the river somewhere near Santa Rosa and pushed on to the Canadian and Colorado. He would have been making for Pueblo, or Denver, dependin' on whether he was aimin' for the Atchison, Topeka, or the Kansas Pacific.'

'The bogus Ed Morgan's calling the shots,' Will said. 'Staying on the east bank of the river puts the herd deeper into the Llano. Way I see it, that feller—'

'Murphy,' Cassie said. 'I told you, I listened to their talk.'

Will nodded. 'Well, if I'm right, this Murphy'll be talkin' to the trail boss and suggestin' they let the cattle gradually drift east. That's away from the river. The stampede'll come when they're in the middle of a nowhere that's as hot as Hades.'

'How?' Bobbie Lee said. 'Sangster's out of it, Van Gelderen's forced to keep his head down. That leaves Cleet and Murphy. You reckon two of 'em can start a stampede, in broad daylight, with eagle-eyed, experienced riders swarming all around that herd?'

'Somehow they'll manage it,' Cassie said. 'But should we be worrying about that? Didn't you try to talk to the rancher and his trail boss, tell them Van Gelderen's plans? And weren't you looked on with suspicion?'

'You're right, of course,' Bobbie Lee said, listening to the unease in his own voice, agreeing when he wasn't sure he felt that way. 'We've done all we could. Gibb wouldn't listen, so now we go about our business.'

'That business,' Will Blunt said, 'has in part been accomplished. Sangster murdered Ed

Morgan. Thanks to Cassie, he's floating face down in the Pecos and heading south. Murphy's leading Gibb and his herd into the wilderness, but that's no concern of ours. Cleet put a hole in your shoulder – you'll get over it. That leaves Van Gelderen.'

'It does,' Cassie said. 'He killed Jason, he wants Bobbie Lee dead for reasons we can only guess at – and having recently escaped from his clutches, I'm surprised you haven't yet asked me where he is.'

Still uneasy, Bobbie Lee flicked his cigarette away and watched it fall sparkling into the water.

'All right,' he said. 'Where is he?'

'The camp was some way north of here. That put the Llano to the west. They were talking around the camp-fire – that's how I got onto Sangster. Nothing was said about Van Gelderen's plans, but from where we'd ended up I'd say his intentions were clear.'

'You figure he's going to use one of those gullies in the escarpment as a way up onto the Llano?'

'If he is,' Will Blunt said, 'that ties in with my notion of Murphy letting the herd drift east. Takes it closer to Van Gelderen, gives him a ringside seat when the fireworks start.'

'Fireworks?'

Will grinned at Bobbie Lee. 'It'll take a six-shooter's full load and then some to get cattle running in that heat.'

That picture was contemplated for a few silent minutes as they paid attention to their coffee. When the last cup had been drained and the dregs disposed of, Bobbie Lee began stowing the gear while Will kicked earth over the fire. He moved with reasonable ease. He was happy with the way his shoulder was healing, and from time to time slipped his left arm out of the sling, flexing his fingers. Improving – but it would be days before he could say it was back to normal.

Nevertheless he was mobile, he had a good right hand – and they knew for sure where Van Gelderen had last been seen. As to his intentions, they'd made an educated guess. OK, that might not be enough, Bobbie Lee thought, but what else did they have to go on – and did it matter? Van Gelderen was going to be in at the kill, that was certain; no matter how he went about it, they knew where he'd finish up. With nothing better to do they could retrace the route Cassie had taken when she rode to freedom, locate the camp-fire where she'd been held. Van Gelderen would be there, or he wouldn't. If they were too late, they'd follow him up onto the Llano. . . .

'You know,' he said, when they were all by their horses, preparing to mount, 'what we told Gibb may have fallen on deaf ears, but it doesn't take away responsibility. We know damn well what Van Gelderen's going to do – and, when you think about it, therein lies the answer.'

'Go on, Bobbie Lee,' Cassie said, one foot in a stirrup. 'Unburden your soul. Tell us what we must do.'

'Getting rid of Van Gelderen solves all problems,' Bobbie Lee said, and saw Blunt nod slowly.

'With him gone, d'you think Murphy or Cleet are going to give a damn about Gibb and his herd? Of course they're not. Remove Van Gelderen, let them know the job's been done, and they'll turn away and ride home.'

'Easy, when you think about it,' Blunt said. 'And, as we've always been after Van Gelderen, the answer's always been there for us to see.'

'All we've got to do,' Bobbie Lee said, 'is get to Van Gelderen before his *compadres* stampede the herd.'

Cassie grinned. 'My turn to contribute some wisdom: if downing Van Gelderen has always been the answer, why the hell are we standing here talking?'

They pushed north without any fears of meeting trouble on the way, convinced Van Gelderen's eyes and intentions lay in the other direction: at some time he would leave the campsite where Cassie had been held captive and make his way up onto the Llano; they would ride hard hoping that the outlaw would see no need for haste and so linger long enough for them to catch him with his pants down.

They made good time. After an hour they stopped to give the horses a breather. Another hour of riding saw them ready for a second halt. Cassie trotted her pony up to join Bobbie Lee.

'I guess you realize we've crossed the trail you and Pa took from the hollow.'

'A half-hour ago. So how much further to that campsite?'

'I'd guess another hour. We're riding steady. This little pony was pushing hard when I was heading south to save your worthless hide.'

He chuckled. 'Stay with me. Tell me if I lose the way.'

'With this moon?'

'Mm. I was thinking about that. Who's in most danger, us or Van Gelderen?'

'If he's still in camp, he's sleeping.'

'Or waiting for Sangster to return with news of my death.'

'No. Surely Sangster would go back to the herd, rejoin Cleet?'

'Maybe. But anyway, them splitting up helps us. If Sangster's missed by one of them, the assumption will be that he's with the other.'

They took the second break, Cassie using some of the precious water to rinse trail dust from her face, Bobbie Lee and Will smoking contentedly as the horses grazed. Then, after some ten minutes, they pushed on.

Despite their confidence, as more time passed nerves began to jangle. They knew they were steadily drawing closer to their objective. Constantly now they were looking ahead for the faint glow of a fire, sniffing the air for the scent of woodsmoke; listening for the whicker of a tethered horse that had caught the sound of their approach.

Cassie had taken the lead. Bobbie Lee was behind her, Will Blunt some thirty yards back. To the north and west the canyon-riven escarpment sloping up to the Llano Estacado was a dark and forbidding bulk against the bright skies. The trail was snaking north across terrain that was mostly flat, but from time to time the way ahead was obscured by a low rise, or straggling stands of parched trees. On those occasions the bright moon cast long shadows; it was ideal bushwhack territory. And it was in a stand of trees just like any of those they passed that Cassie had been held.

The moon cast shadows where bushwackers might lurk, but it also helped the likely targets.

'Bobbie Lee!'

Cassie's call was soft, but urgent.

She reined in hard, dust rising as she half turned her pony and looked back.

'In those trees, I think I saw a flash of metal—'

Even as she called the warning, Bobbie Lee was moving.

'Ride for it!' he yelled, and spun his horse.

He was still dragging the big sorrel's head around and urging it off the trail when, up ahead, the gunman's position was exposed by a bright orange muzzle flash that lit up the trees. A second later came the crack of the shot. Cursing, Bobbie Lee ducked low. The bullet whispered over his head.

Behind him, Will Blunt grunted.

A second shot cracked. Bobbie Lee tore after Cassie into the deep cover of yet more trees. Ducking into the shadows, skin prickling, he flicked a glance backward. Will Blunt was slumped in the saddle, his chin on his chest. As Bobbie Lee watched in horror, Blunt fell sideways and toppled from his horse to land on the trail in a crumpled heap.

Anger boiled in Bobbie Lee like water in a hot sulphur spring. He snapped two shots off in the direction of the gunman. They were wild, poorly aimed but almost at once he heard the rattle of hooves, fast retreating. Then he was down off the sorrel and running through the trees towards the still figure lying on the trail.

SEVENTEEN

When Bobbie Lee had looked on the trio riding out of Beattie's Halt as a strangely mismatched group, nothing in his mind could have prepared him for the sombre duo now leading a third horse west. They rode through the early dawn light towards the Llano Estacado and a confrontation with rancher Harlan Gibb, and ever present in their minds was that third horse and the empty saddle with its stirrups tied up.

After the fateful ambush they had spent the rest of the night at the outlaws' old campsite, relighting their fire and huddling around the heat as much for spiritual comfort as for the warmth of the crackling flames.

Will Blunt was dead because, when Bobbie Lee ducked out of the way, the slug he knew was intended for him had whined over his head and drilled Cassie's father through the heart. Will had died in the saddle, and knew nothing of the indignity of falling like a sack into the dust of the trail.

Throughout that night no recriminations were

made, no hint of blame cast or acknowledged. Talk was mostly of Will's past life, and after much poignant reminiscing they reached the question of what they should do now that he had passed away. Cassie wanted him buried back at the Halt. Bobbie Lee agreed with her, but their determination to exact a just revenge on Van Gelderen left them torn between two courses.

They could return to the Halt, or they could press on with the hunt for Van Gelderen. But if they decided on the latter, what were they to do with the body of Will Blunt?

In the end, after much soul searching, they knew what they must do; what Will Blunt would want them to do. And so with what tools they had and then with their bare hands they scraped a shallow depression, laid him to rest, and over the man they both loved they heaped rocks that would both mark the spot and keep away the prowling wolves.

Then, drained by emotion but determined to carry on, they again sat by the fire and considered their options.

It was Cassie who had pointed the way with a comment that came out of the blue. As the long night had dragged on, the talk had turned from sadness to more general nostalgia. Suddenly, something Cassie said startled and saddened Bobbie Lee. He knew that what she had told him gave them an argument that would at once discredit Murphy, and convince Gibb that they were telling the truth. He also knew that if Cassie had mentioned it sooner, or if he had remembered what she had said during the discussion before they left the Halt, Will Blunt might still be alive.

One look into Cassie's eyes told him that it was a thought that would always return to haunt her.

By the time they reached the Staked Plains and caught up with the herd it was strung out in a mile-long column and the heat was enough to beat a man out of the saddle. The sun burned down out of a searing white sky stretching to horizons that shimmered like water. Dust was a salty, choking cloud. Riders pulled bandannas up over mouth and nostrils and squinted ahead through watering, narrowed eyes. The cattle moved reluctantly, plodding onward with swaying, drooping heads, and drag riders were working their socks off bringing stragglers back to the column.

As Bobbie Lee led the way at an angle towards the lead riders his eyes were searching for sign of the man in buckskins, the lean figure of Cleet with his marshal's badge. Cleet he did not see. Murphy was some hundred yards in the van, riding with the trail boss, Hobbs.

Then Harlan Gibb came cantering across from the chuck wagon. A short, fat cigar was in the corner of his mouth, his hat pulled down, a dusty red bandanna loose around his neck. His first quick glance took in the horse with its empty saddle. He looked once with keen appreciation at Cassie, then swung in alongside Bobbie Lee.

'You changed your mind about talking to the marshal?'

'Some things that happen change a man forever,' Bobbie Lee said. 'You met the grey-haired feller who should be riding that horse. He got us out of a tight situation using a gambler's pistol. Will Blunt was my friend, and this woman's father. Last night he was gunned down by the man called Van Gelderen. The third death in as many days – and you're playing along with these killers.'

'Van Gelderen again.' Gibb chewed on the cigar. 'A phantom, a ghost rider.'

'He's out there, and he's no ghost.'

'What about the man with the long rifle? Earp came back without him.'

'The name's a joke, it's Cleet, not Earp. Put your question to him. The answer might be interesting, but it's sure to be a lie. The man with the rifle was Sangster. He was sent by Van Gelderen to kill me and Will Blunt. Things didn't work out for him. Right now he's taking a watery ride to south to the Rio Grande.'

'You killed him?'

'He was taken care of. How it happened is neither here nor there because I'm about to ruin your day – or maybe save the rest of this drive, and you from financial ruin – by discrediting your so-called guide.'

'You weren't able to do that in your earlier visit, so why now?'

'Because now I'm able to back up my words with hard proof. Bring the so-called Ed Morgan over here, Gibb. Let's see what he's got to say for himself.'

'I don't take orders from anyone, but especially not from you.'

'Not even to save your herd?'

Gibb took the cigar from his mouth.

'There's a man up there with my trail boss. I hired him as a guide, and I've seen nothing to suggest he doesn't know his job. Marshal Earp is riding tirelessly' – Gibb waved an arm in a sweeping arc – 'keeping his eyes peeled for trouble. So far he's not put a foot wrong—'

'They've been with you less than a full day.'

'—yet you expect me to believe those two men are fixing to start a stampede under the eyes of a dozen or so—'

'That third man, the ghost, is out there somewhere. The man with a chip on his shoulder and with a grudge that's an unbearable weight.'

Gibb shook his head. 'Van Gelderen. I don't know the name, I've yet to see this ghostly figure.'

'Forget him, for now. Go get your guide. Or send someone for him. Let's get to the bottom of this.'

'I told you, I—'

'Don't take orders. Yes, I know.' Bobbie Lee looked across at Cassie, then grinned without humour at the rancher and abruptly put spurs to his horse.

He galloped hard for the front of the herd. Gibb yelled after him. Then his angry hails stopped and, with a flicker of amusement, Bobbie Lee wondered how Cassie had reacted. She'd reloaded the little Remington. He could just imagine her smiling

137

sweetly as she pointed those twin barrels at the rancher's angry countenance.

The trail boss, Hobbs, was the first to spot him.

'Christ,' he said as Bobbie Lee rode up, 'here comes the bad smell.'

The other man, the one calling himself Murphy, twisted in the saddle to see what was going on. In that instant it was as if a veil had fallen across his blue eyes. His expression became virtually unreadable but, if Bobbie Lee had been asked for an opinion, he would have said that the man was badly shaken.

'You know who I am?' Bobbie Lee asked.

'Janson.'

'Yeah, that was probably an easy one. And I recall you sitting with Van Gelderen in my saloon, so I guess he would have roughed in things you'd need to know to carry off this deception. Names, and so on.'

'There's no deception,' Hobbs said.

'So Gibb said. All I'm asking for is proof, one way or another. That can be done in seconds if your man comes over to where your boss is talking to a sweet lady who's just lost her pa.'

The buckskin-clad guide shook his head. 'I'm Ed Morgan. You were gone fifteen years. I was ten years old when you left. What the hell do you know?'

'I know you've done some homework, but I don't think it's enough. Come on, humour me. Let's go talk to that young lady.'

'There's no call—'

Hobbs cut him off. 'Do it, Ed. Settle this, once and for all.'

The guide's jaw went white as he clenched his teeth. Then he shook his head irritably, and swung his horse around. Bobbie Lee rode with him back to Harlan Gibb. He was aware that Hobbs was following on behind.

Gibb and Cassie were indeed chatting; when Bobbie Lee rode off, she must have calmed him with sweet talk rather than the little pistol's threat. As the three riders approached, Gibb watched with interest, and Bobbie Lee wondered if Cassie had also managed to sow seeds of doubt in the lean rancher's mind.

Dust was a drifting cloud as the riders came together and bunched. Bobbie Lee looked at Cassie, saw the understanding and deep anger in her eyes.

'You know this feller?'

'Never saw him before now.'

'This is Ed Morgan.'

Cassie shook her head. 'Ed Morgan was a dear friend, and he's dead.'

Harlan Gibb moved restlessly in the saddle.

'This is going round in circles. Where's the hard proof you mentioned?'

'Your man's real name is Murphy,' Bobbie Lee said, and silenced the man's quick denial with a raised hand while his eyes held the rancher's gaze. 'He recognized me but, hell, who wouldn't? And we saw him in Beattie's Halt anyway, so that was easy. But if he's Ed Morgan, not Murphy, then his memory should go back more than a couple of days.'

'That's fair enough,' Gibb said. 'Go on.'

Bobbie Lee looked at the man in buckskins.

'You recognize this woman?'

The guide sneered. 'My work's taken me to southern Texas, you think I know everyone—'

'Two years,' Bobbie Lee said. 'That's the length of time you've been gone. A couple of minutes ago you told me you were ten years old when I left Beattie's Halt, but you recognized me straight off. You knew this woman for all but the last couple of years – so, tell me, tell us all – what's her name?'

'You expect me to remember the name of every woman I've ever met?'

'Cassie,' Bobbie Lee said, 'show that Henry rifle to Gibb.'

The rifle flashed in the sunlight as Cassie drew it like a sword from its boot and handed it to the rancher.

He took it, looked at with approval, turned it in his hands. When he looked up, his gaze had hardened.

'Recognize this, Morgan?' he said. Suddenly he was placing a distasteful emphasis on the name, and Bobbie Lee felt an instant surge of relief.

The guide shrugged. 'A Henry. Forerunner of the Winchester. A good rifle—'

'It's got some writing on it,' Gibb said. 'Beautifully engraved. It says "For Cassie Blunt, love always – Ed Morgan".' He held the rifle up, turned it in the sunlight so that the guide could see the engraving.

140

'I guess it slipped my mind—'

'Bobbie Lee!'

It was Cassie's urgent warning that turned every man's eyes towards her, then sent them looking in the direction of her outstretched arm. On the far side of the strung-out column of cattle, Cleet was riding close to the herd between Gibb's men riding point and swing. He had something in his hands that he was whirling overhead like a rope. From it, sparks were flying. As they watched, he took a last wide swing and sent the object hurtling over the cattle. It seemed to hang in the air, then dropped and settled over a pair of long horns. At once, a series of crackling explosions split the hot day's searing torpor.

'Chinese firecrackers,' Bobbie Lee yelled. And suddenly there was pandemonium as the lead steers broke and ran.

EIGHTEEN

The timing was wrong, the placing of the fire-crackers done in haste and without thought.

That realization, added to the knowledge that he and Cassie by their actions had pushed Cleet into making those mistakes, rode with Bobbie Lee like a bright beacon of triumph as the group of riders spurred their mounts towards the shelter of the chuck wagon.

Gibb went ahead of them, leaving the stampeding herd to his men. He kept a firm hold on Cassie's Henry, levered a shell into the breech and never let his aim waver as he forced Murphy to ride with them to the wagon. There he dismounted, and with a few curt words handed the unmasked outlaw over to the glowering, Derby-hatted cook.

'I guess I owe you,' Gibb said, as Bobbie Lee drew rein, his voice raised over the thunder of the running herd, the shrill yips of his men and the crackle of exploding firecrackers.

'Us, and Cleet's panic. He watched what was going on with Murphy, placed those firecrackers in

142

the wrong place and saved your herd. Cleet set it running in the wrong direction. It'll end up back where it started, on the banks of the Pecos.'

Gibb grinned. 'Yeah, with that in mind we're letting them run themselves out. They'll rest for a day, I get a second chance of making Colorado.'

'You had any thoughts about Van Gelderen?'

'The ghost?' Gibb smiled ruefully. 'Why?'

'If I've been right once, I could be right twice. That man who's staying out of your way is behind this stampede. I'd like to know why.'

Murphy had been forced off his feet by the cantankerous, short-fused cook and was sitting with his back to one of the wagon wheels. The cook's shotgun was lying across a box, cocked, pointing at the outlaw.

Gibb tossed the Henry to Cassie, then turned to Murphy.

'You were hiding under another man's name,' he said. 'What about Van Gelderen?'

Murphy's face was sullen. 'He made it up. His name's Vern Hedger.'

'Christ, why didn't I think of him?' Gibb said. He shook his head when he looked at Bobbie Lee. 'Hedger had a wife and kid, a section on my land where he ran a small herd of dairy cows using my water; that was on fine grassland along a fork of the Colorado. Then something went wrong. His wife left him, moved into San Angelo with the kid. Hedger took to drink. When he began losing money, he rode out one night and stole some of my best cows.'

'So you turned him off your land?'

'Gave him the choice,' Gibb said. 'Pack his bags, or get his neck stretched for rustling.'

Bobbie Lee was still in the saddle, Cassie astride her pony a few yards away as the dust kicked up by the hooves of two thousand running animals rolled like the smoke of battle and rose like a pall to mask the hot sun.

But the vast cloud was drifting south with the running cattle and, but for sheer serendipity, for Bobbie Lee that could have been the wrong way. The chuck wagon and the small group of onlookers were left in bright clean air, outlined like painted figures against the rolling dun backcloth. The man watching in anger and disbelief from the edge of the Staked Plains' escarpment had a clear view that offered an opportunity he dare not refuse, and sent his hand reaching to his saddle boot for his Winchester rifle.

The gunshot went unheard. Out of the chaos all around them the bullet came like an unseen messenger of death. The aim was sure, the bullet flew straight and true, but once again a head moved and one man's life was saved. This time it was a horse that changed position and foiled an attempted murder. For some reason – animal instinct, or hearing sharper than any human's – Bobbie Lee's big sorrel jerked up its head. The slug took it in its graceful throat. It was dying as it fell.

NINETEEN

It was midday when they picked up Vern Hedger's trail.

They had stayed with the chuck wagon until Harlan Gibb decided it was time to take it trundling south. Then, with Bobbie Lee astride Will Blunt's skinny blue roan, they bade their farewells and rode towards the escarpment.

With the herd running towards the edge of the hard pan and the grassland beyond, the dust had settled and a mind-numbing silence had fallen over the Staked Plains. It was as if all life had been sucked away, and the very air itself had thickened and was bearing down on their heads under the weight of the intense heat.

They had drunk their fill, replenished water bottles, soaked their bandannas and done everything they could to ease their way as they set out across that scorching wilderness – yet still they struggled. And when, a mere fifteen minutes later, they caught the glint of a brass .44 cartridge lying where it had fallen, saw the sharp-cut hoof marks in the baked earth and followed that trail with their eyes into the shimmering heat-haze – the task they had set themselves seemed beyond their capabilities.

They took a drink while they could. Bobbie Lee splashed water into his hat for the horses. He knew Cassie was watching him; knew she was thinking of the way ahead, the water they could carry compared with what they would need.

'If he can do it,' Cassie said, 'so can we.'

'Sure. What's a spell of warm weather to folks from Beattie's Halt?'

'Is there water out there, Bobbie Lee?'

'Oh yes. I think Hedger knows that.'

'So he didn't need Murphy if he knew that. He could have snuggled up to Harlan Gibb and led the herd himself if he'd changed his face as well as his name.'

Bobbie Lee chuckled at the thought of Hedger growing a beard and wearing an eye-patch. He wiped his face with the damp bandanna, then sobered and pointed north.

'Far as I recall, Hedger won't get a drink that don't come out of a warm tin bottle for at least another hundred miles. About then, the Rio Hondo forks off the Pecos. If it was me, that's the way to go. If he heads for that water hole I think is out there in the middle of the Plains, he'll be more than fifty miles to the east of the lush green grass and fighting to stay alive.'

'Then why do it? Why not head for the river?'

'Who can tell what drives a man? Harlan Gibb

said something went wrong. Maybe that slip inside Hedger's brain warped his entire way of thinking. A normal man formulating plans would pay some thought to what happens afterwards. Maybe Hedger couldn't see that far. Maybe he could and did, but when things went wrong his loose thinking took another jar.'

'A long answer,' Cassie said, 'but even if some of it's right it leaves us chasing a man who's riding blind.'

'So we chase him until he runs out of space or time.'

'And then?'

Bobbie Lee planted his damp hat on his head and climbed onto the roan.

'That's about the worst question you could ask. Cold-blooded killing is what Hedger deserves, but that's something I've not done in the past and I know I can't do it now.'

'If he fights,' Cassie said, 'that makes it easy.'

'Killing him is already justifiable. That would make it easier to stomach.'

There was no more talk.

They pressed on, acutely aware of the hundred hard miles that separated them from that water hole, always harbouring the forlorn hope that they would overtake Hedger but knowing full well that pursuit across the Llano Estacado would always resemble a race between snails.

Their water was rationed, several small sips each hour, more for the horses who were bearing the brunt of the hard going. Bobbie Lee reckoned they were covering no more than eight miles in each hour; by mid-afternoon that put them some forty miles from the start, sixty miles from the water-hole.

Towards dusk, with the sun a fierce orange ball over the purple hills to the west and another thirty miles under their belts, something plucked Bobbie Lee's hat from his head. Cassie caught the wink of the distant muzzle flash. She opened her mouth to cry out and turned the paint towards Bobbie Lee. Then she felt her mind freeze as she realized what she had done. Even as she gasped, there was a solid, fleshy smack. That second bullet took the paint pony behind the left shoulder. Shot through the heart, it died on its feet and dropped without a sound.

TWENTY

'The sorrel was luck, the paint deliberate. He went for mine first and aimed high. But now we know he's going for the horses, and you gave him a target he couldn't miss.'

After the second fatal shot, silence had settled over the plains. The sun was almost down, the Llano Estacado an endless moonscape of rock and scrub bathed in eerie red light. Bobbie Lee and Cassie were huddled behind the warm body of the dead paint pony. Will Blunt's blue roan was some yards away, reins trailing. It was exposed and vulnerable. One carefully placed shot by the distant gunman would leave them on foot in the middle of a wilderness and there was nothing they could do to stop him.

'I know,' Cassie said. 'I knew as soon as I turned.' Her laugh was bitter. 'I was so sure the shot was coming I almost lifted my left leg up out of the way.'

'Well,' Bobbie Lee said, 'he's out there now, maybe looking through the sights with his finger on the trigger, but it's getting dark. If he holds off for the next half hour, we've got away with it; we've got one horse between us, and we'll use it as best we can.'

'How?'

'Let me think about it,' Bobbie Lee said, and suddenly his mind was busy turning disaster into good fortune. 'Hedger's been riding all day,' he said. 'He's hot; he's tired; he thinks he's got the upper hand; thinks he's stopped us in our tracks. What he'll do is bed down for the night – and that gives us a chance. When he's asleep, we'll ride straight past him.'

'Pa's blue roan can't carry two of us,' Cassie said.

'We'll do it this way,' Bobbie Lee said. 'Thirty miles to go, so we'll take turns jogging and riding through the cool of the night.'

'But you said yourself Hedger's out there. If we travel in a straight line, we're liable to fall over him.'

'The moon's rising in clear skies. Hedger will be dead to the world. We'll see his horse from a distance and stay well away, circle around him. He'll never know we've gone past. When he finds out, it'll be too late.'

Cassie was watching him, her eyes puzzled.

'I've been listening, and as plans go it's not bad at all. But this is the man we're hunting. So the question is, if we find him, why go past?'

'Yeah, I thought you'd get around to that,'

Bobbie Lee said. He sighed. 'I told you before, I've never killed in cold blood. I guess there's a side to me that demands fair play. I never threw down on an unarmed man, never drew my pistol first, so any man I came up against always knew he had the edge.'

'So taking a sleeping man, at night, is against some personal code?'

'That's about it.'

Cassie grinned. 'Don't be apologetic, Bobbie Lee. I like it. More than that, my opinion of you has soared, and God knows it was already sky high. And, like I said, as plans go it's pretty good. I can see the beauty of it now: we go riding past, and in the morning when Hedger arrives at the water-hole and prepares to pick us off as we ride in out of the sun—'

'We'll be there, waiting. He'll be caught out in the open, and that's where it'll end.'

The moon was high and bright. Alongside the lather-strung, doggedly trotting blue roan, Bobbie Lee was jogging economically with one hand resting light on the cantle. Despite the cooler air, his face was wet. Every so often he used the now stiff bandanna to clear the salt sweat from his eyes. When he looked up he could see Cassie's chin dropping to her chest as she swayed in the saddle, and he knew she was dozing.

Well, that was OK. Bobbie Lee was tall enough to see some way into the distance. The air was mostly crystal clear, but close to the cooling ground a thin night mist lay like a white blanket stretching the length and breadth of the plains. He knew that the eerie mist rising from the cooling earth to turn a watcher cross-eyed with looking could work for them, or against them: they could blunder across the sleeping Hedger, or ride straight on by without seeing, or being seen.

In the end it worked out somewhat differently.

Cassie's soft warning alerted Bobbie Lee, and when he started at the sound he was amazed to realize she was now awake and he'd been dozing as he ran.

'Over there, Bobbie Lee.'

She reined in the roan. Off to the east, no more than fifty yards away, he saw the dark shape of a horse standing hip-shot with mist up to its hocks, sleeping in the moonlight. Close by, a pencil-thin column of smoke arose from a dying fire. And, despite the mist, Bobbie Lee could see the outline of a man lying on the hard ground, wrapped in blankets, his covered head resting on his saddle.

'Glory be,' he said softly. 'I'll be double damned if we ain't going to make it.'

'Steady now, don't count chickens just yet,' Cassie said. 'So, do we circle wide, or chance it?'

'Keep going. At a walk. But hand me that Henry.'

In the leaden silence that was the dead of night they managed to move silently: a woman on a lathered horse, whispering to calm the animal; a man walking in its shadow, a rifle gleaming in his one good arm. Far off a coyote howled mournfully, and Bobbie Lee knew that sounds like that would lull the sleeping outlaw. The one sound he didn't want to hear was a whicker from the man's dozing horse, and so he walked on by with his heart hammering somewhere up between his chest and his mouth and within him the urge to break into a run and get the hell out of there.

Fifty yards beyond Vern Hedger the sweat was streaming down his face and, hoarsely, he told Cassie that it looked like they'd made it.

'All we've got to hope now,' she said, 'is that he's heading for that water-hole. You just had what might be your best chance, and passed it up. I hope you don't live to regret it.'

The water-hole was a fringe of wilting grey-green cottonwoods and cactus marking a flat area of shiny gunmetal that glittered like ice in the light of the approaching dawn. It was a mile away. If they stumbled across those remaining barren yards, they had made it. But strength had gone with the last of the water, will-power alone was stopping them from lying down, curling up and dying – and Bobbie Lee wasn't too sure if he had much of that commodity left to draw on.

After they'd sneaked past Hedger, he had worked it so that he did most of the running, Cassie most of the riding. She was slumped in the saddle now, peering ahead with bleary eyes, her flaxen hair straggly and matted with sweat. The blue roan was moving at a walk. Bobbie Lee hung onto the cantle with his good arm and forced weary legs to take one step, then another, and still another – and always there seemed to be too many steps to be taken to reach the water-hole; always it seemed that the beckoning glitter of cold water was not drawing nearer, but receding.

'We get there,' he said hoarsely, 'we'll have time to drink our fill, freshen up, get into position.'

'If the water's fit to drink.'

'Yeah,' he said, 'you go ahead and cheer me up.'

Cassie chuckled. 'If there's dead carcasses poisoning the water, we can suck on a fat cactus. We'll survive. And we'll be ready when Hedger rides in.'

Then they cut out the talk and concentrated on the last mile.

It took them what Bobbie Lee estimated was half an hour. Then, between sand and stone, parched grass sprouted. The grass became green. It was moist with dew. The pony had been moving with a lightened step and its head lifted high for fifteen of those last thirty minutes. Now it tried to break into a trot. Cassie held it back, talking to it through cracked lips, keeping the reins taut. Still its pace quickened. Stumbling to keep up, Bobbie Lee let them go. He watched Cassie bouncing weakly in the saddle as the roan broke into a trot. Then horse and rider were plunging down the basin's slight incline. He saw them reach the water's edge, heard the splash, a tantalizing liquid sound that had been haunting his waking dreams for most of the night. He saw the water's flat surface break, the widening circle of ripples. . . .

Bobbie Lee could smell it, taste it, from fifty yards away. The blue roan was standing spread legged, head down. Cassie was on her knees, splashing water over her face and shoulders.

And then Bobbie Lee was there with the horse and the woman. There were no rotting carcasses. The water was fresh and clear and cold. He fell to his knees, gasped at the shock, leaned forward and drank.

'Goddamn,' Bobbie Lee said after a while, still on his knees, water dribbling from his unshaven chin and cupped hands. 'That must be the best drink I've tasted since we left The Last Water-hole.'

'Make the most of it,' a hard voice said. 'That drink you tasted was your last.'

When Bobbie turned his head, he saw the lean man he had known as Van Gelderen standing back on the edge of the cottonwoods. The conchos in his hat-band glittered. His black clothing was caked with dust. One of his six-guns was held nonchalantly at his side.

'I suppose your horse is hid in the trees. Where'd you get the other one?'

'You think I'd risk crossing the Llano without a spare? I bought it from a trader taking fifty head down into Texas.'

'And the man sleeping by the fire? A dummy?'

'Rocks, and a blanket.' Hedger grinned. 'The extra saddle came with the horse.'

He'd moved away from the cottonwoods as they spoke and was standing on the basin's lip. Close. A mere twenty yards away. Bobbie Lee climbed out of the water and contrived to put some distance between him and Cassie. She did the same, stealing another yard away to his right as she stood up.

Their scheming didn't fool Hedger. He was watching with a cynical grin.

Gives him two targets spaced out – but so what? Bobbie Lee wondered. The man had the drop on them. Cassie's Henry was back in the saddle boot. His own six-gun was in its holster – but was he fast enough? Hedger would have managed to get some sleep. Bobbie Lee was wrung out, leg-weary, his left shoulder stiff and the arm back in the sling. He'd draw with his right – if he made the try – but he'd be off balance, and weariness would make him sluggish.

The cogitating became of no importance.

'Unbuckle your gunbelt,' Hedger said, 'let it drop, then kick it into the water.'

Bobbie Lee looked at Cassie. There was something in her eyes. He held her gaze for a moment, searching for meaning. Then he slipped the belt's tongue out of the buckle and let it fall.

'Into the water.'

Bobbie Lee complied. The belt and six-gun splashed into the water hole.

'Why?' he asked. 'I can understand your hatred of Harlan Gibb, the twisted reasoning behind it –

but why my boy, why me?'

'You've already been told. Murphy was close by and listening when Smoky gave you the reason.'

'Smoky, the cook? Remind me.'

'San Angelo.'

'Ah.' Bobbie Lee nodded. 'A gunfight, he said. I remember it, but I was on my way out of town before the man I shot dead hit the ground.'

'You were in the middle of Main Street when the guns began blasting,' Hedger said, and his face was tight with bleak memories. 'Folk had gathered to watch. The man you killed managed to get a shot off.'

'I always gave them a break.'

'That shot went wide. It took my little girl in the right eye, killed her stone dead.'

Bobbie Lee heard Cassie gasp.

'I guess you were trying to tell me something at breakfast in The Last Water-hole,' he said. 'You couldn't understand why I was facing the man who'd killed my son, and doing nothing about it. I knew his name, knew exactly where he was, whereas you lost track of me. . . .' He thought for a moment. 'You found me in the end – but was that pure luck?'

'Sure. I had a job to do that took me to Beattie's Halt. I rode in – and there you were.'

'Why let me live after you killed Jason?'

'I wanted you to feel some of the pain I'd been carrying with me for years – and there was that job, I had a score to settle with Harlan Gibb. I knew you'd come after me. Killing you could wait.'

'Bobbie Lee!'

Her voice was urgent. He flicked his gaze to the right. His skin prickled. While he and Hedger had been locked in conversation, Cassie had worked the little Remington over-and-under out of her boot. It was glittering in the strengthening light. As he turned his head, she threw it underhand towards him, hard and fast.

It was classic misdirection. Hedger had heard the shout. His eyes flicked to Cassie. Reacting when he saw she was armed, he began to lift his six-gun and swing towards her.

The Remington spun towards Bobbie Lee. It was coming from his right. His left arm was in a sling. A catch with his right hand would be awkward. Instinctively, he brought his left forearm off his chest, pointing his empty hand as if firing from the hip. The white triangle of the sling tightened from wrist to shoulder. The pistol hit the tight flat cloth, a small bird fluttering against a net. It began to fall. Bobbie Lee grabbed it with his right hand.

Twenty yards away on the lip of the basin, Hedger's teeth drew back in a snarl. He was fast. He'd turned when he saw Cassie with the Remington. Now he swung back, brought the six-gun to bear on Bobbie Lee.

But Cassie's cunning move meant the outlaw was always going to be that fraction too slow. He was too slow swinging towards Cassie. Too slow reacting to the bewildering change and switching his aim to Bobbie Lee.

And before Cassie flipped the little Remington to Bobbie Lee, she'd cocked the hammer.

The crack of the pistol in the dawn air was the snapping of a thin twig. A black spot appeared in the centre of Hedger's forehead. His finger jerked on the trigger. The blast of the six-gun split the dawn air. The bullet smacked into the water.

Vern Hedger's eyes rolled back in his head. The whites gleamed like milk, the eyes of a blind man – or a man already dead. His legs buckled. He hit the ground on his knees, flopped onto his face and lay still.

In the sudden, deathly silence, Bobbie Lee could hear Cassie breathing. He looked at her. Her cheeks were flushed, her eyes bright.

'You OK?' he said.

'I am now.'

'You're too clever for your own good.'

Her chuckle was a rich gurgle.

'I know. And d'you know what we're going to do now?'

'Tell me.'

'We're going to get that horse Hedger left in the desert. Then we're going all the way back for my pa. We're going to pull those rocks off him, and we're going to take him back to the Halt and give him a *proper* burial.'

'And Hedger?'

'We do the same for him.' She shook her head. 'It's ironic, Bobbie Lee. When we're finished today and the sun's going down, we'll drink to my pa's memory in your saloon, The Last Water-hole. But for Van Gelderen, Vern Hedger, whatever you care to call him, the last water hole he'll ever see is here – and *he'll* be here forever.'

'There but for the grace of God. . . .' Bobbie Lee said fervently. 'Come on, Cass, we've got work to do.